I0629469

LARCENY OF THE HEART II: THE AMERICAN DREAM

A Novel By

Maxwell Penn

Art design by: www.myspace.com/crayonMAFIAGFX

Manufactured and distributed by:

Sincere Communication Group Inc.

511 Avenue of the Americas

Suite# 154

N.Y. N.Y. 10011

Contact: Sincerecommgroup.com

(917) 915-5641

Acknowledgements

First and foremost I'd like to thank the most important group of people in my career; Y O U the reader for purchasing and reading my art. One can't fathom the amount of gratitude I have for all my loyal supporters which can't be expressed in mere words. You make me a world class champion with every page of my work that you read. Thanks are also in order to my big brother Melquan for never letting me stop writing, you were right it does get greater later! Thanks to all the retailers, distributors, vendors and book clubs that show my label mates and I love as well. Peace be upon all my family members: Allah's Nation of God and Earth, the Cheathams, the Clarks, the Hendersons, and the Headleys. Peace to Eternal Mathematics Allah and the team at Sincere Communications Group Inc.

Love and respect to my colleague, fellow S.C.G. label mate and franchise player Frederick Chappel for signing with the winning team! Peace to Lord Kalim Allah, Justice Born Allah, Radi Allah (Sun Wun) and the rest of my Supreme Team Inc. crew. Thanks to my editor Nasira Moor and her staff at Best Part Publishing. One love to my brothers, comrades and colleague's Darkim Be Allah Christ (www.Famelabsmusic.com) Master K-Bar Allah, Venge Mills, El-Sun Wise Allah, Sterlin Gates, Tra Verdejo, Isadore Johnson, A.R. Hilton, Antuan "Thug Love" Sumter, Arlene (Boss lady) Brathwaite and Keith Young of Cook City Publishing. Peace to all thorough bred hustlers around the globe... we make the whole world go around while the squares just live in it! Last however far from least my young soldiers Star Born Mo'kwan Allah, and Nazir Damani Henderson-Banks who are gone yet far too good to ever be forgotten.

Love is love,

Max P. The Sultan of Swagger

CHAPTER ONE

In the distance still about two thousand feet below them, Winsome could see the Statue of Liberty. She got so excited she couldn't help but squeal a little behind her hand as she turned to speak to Gwen in the small spaces between the seats on the giant airplane. "Look over deh so! …The Statue of Liberty…the Statue of Liberty!"

Winsome said it several times in disbelief because it didn't feel real. She didn't feel as though she'd really left her whole life and everything she'd ever known behind. If felt like being in a daydream or a wish and any moment now, reality would smack her awake and she would no longer be on a plane, on her way to New York to live. She'd be back home in Jamaica, without Jean, without her twin sons, without the promise of a new life and adventure before her.

The plane roared and bounced and Winsome hugged Jean tightly. They drifted below the clouds and she prayed thankfully, because that was indeed the reality of what was going to take place that blistering cold December afternoon in 1972. Behind her and Jean, her older sister Gwen's mouth hung open and she sat silent, squeezing Chinaman's arm through the turbulence. They were circling the airport now. Just five minutes later, the plane touched down and they were in America.

Once they all were off the plane, they faced Customs. Winsome's heart was in her belly as she held Peter, her beautiful oldest son. She kissed his head and bounced him rhythmically, more to distract herself than for his benefit. He was calm, blissfully unaware that their passports, bought in the middle of the night, were fake. They had run for their lives and spent a large portion of their entire life's wealth on those papers. When she and Jean-Paul got to the head of the line, they'd find out whether or not the passports they had were worth the paper they were printed on.

Beside her, Jean was fully in his role of the tourist. His chiseled features showed no emotion and she drew strength from his boldness, a false strength she did not feel. He'd stood strong the same way throughout the numerous obstacles they'd been through when, without him, the stress and fear would have broken her. She felt sweat running down her armpits and tingling on her scalp. She bounced the baby harder, hugging him to her, knowing she was trying to shield herself behind his father's power that ran through his veins.

Gwen held Paul, her beloved nephew. The two babies, Peter and Paul, were born only minutes apart. Paul was blessed, kissed by heaven with a certain innate charm that made people protect him, where as Peter seemed to have it hard and usually had to make his own way. They shared the same beautiful face, their father's features graced with her silky complexion and wild curly hair. Everywhere they went, people stopped in awe of them, praising and kissing and cooing with the two babies, who shared their father's couldn't-care-less magnetism. The less attention they paid to people, the more people thirsted to be noticed by them, it seemed.

When the whites ahead of them were passed through, Winsome felt her bowels turn to liquid, the fear creeping up her neck and her arms going numb. Her cowardice shamed her and she held on tighter to her baby, not looking at Jean who she knew would not recognize the pathetic creature standing beside him.

"State your business."

The customs agent looked like he could shoot you in the head without batting an eyelash, if it was in his job description. He didn't appear to have any compassion or ability to be reasoned with because his only concern when that uniform was on his back was his pension. She could not meet his eyes and busied herself by looking for her son's bottle in her burgundy purse. The purse matched her beige wrap dress. She'd put on a little weight since their birth but she knew her man was a prize and she would never let any scallywag outshine her. She kept herself coordinated and pretty, always making sure to pay attention to the little things like the perfume he liked…and the kisses he craved.

"Sir, I am here with my family for work and schooling. We- my two sons, my wife, my brother," Jean-Paul had stepped to the man, standing in front of them and now he moved and pointed to Chinaman, who stood next to Gwen, as he spoke. The Customs man did not look up until then, carefully studying China, whose given name was Paul Chin. China was half pure Chinese, and his chinky eyes, fair skin and hair proved it. His attitude though, was pure Yard, and though the man studied him, he gave the calculated effect of the cool breeze as he played with Peter, who laughed lovingly in Gwen's arms. China couldn't give any less of a damn what the man thought of him and he radiated that where Jean, who was all business, let him know that his word was bond and what he said was law.

The Customs agent had no such convictions in his life. He only saw what he could see with his physical eyes: two absolutely gorgeous young women carrying babies, on the arms of two young lions, carrying their babies. Their small waists and curvy, childbearing hips lay promise to many, many more - they promised a dynasty. He thought of the fights he'd run from; the things he'd come to just accept; his tough, angry, square yellow-skinned wife and her daughter and the pen he'd closed himself in, always playing it safe and it was too much. He stamped the passports with all of his wasted might and waved them through. "Next!"

A wave of relief settled over them as they made their way through all the pedestrian traffic and picked their luggage up from the baggage claim area. Then, outside on to the cab stand they went. Everyone except for Gwen was getting their first taste of what a real New York winter was all about. Gwen had come to New York first to work, years ago. She tried to tell Winnie, but you can't reason with a woman in love. The US to Gwen was cold, ugly and harsh. She hated it compared to their beautiful sunny island.

The most clothes any one had on were dungarees and long sleeve button ups. Their clothes weren't enough for the freezing thirty-two degree weather with the wind chill factor for that day making it feel more like eighteen degrees. The approximate fifty degree disparity in climate from when they were in Ocho Rios was enormous. It didn't matter - the difference may as well have been one hundred degrees. On a breezy Caribbean night, the absolute coldest weather any one of them except for Gwen had experienced was about sixty five degrees. She held sweet, sweet baby Peter, her one true love in this life, as she summoned a cab.

It began to snow and everyone except for Gwen just stood there awestruck, caught up in the moment. Winsome actually had her mouth wide open. She wanted to taste the flakes as if they had flavor. At first it was as though, to Gwen's astonishment, the idiot started trying to sniff them. Then, she stuck her tongue out and tried to taste them.

"Winnie, stop acting like a pure Id-i-ot gal don't you know about pollution here in New York?" Gwen was embarrassed; Winsome was acting juvenile, and she didn't want her to draw attention and act like a dunce.

While the women bantered, Jean and China both hugged each other energetically, slapping each other on the back hard, with a strength that could have broke a weak man's spine. They had both cheated death and had made it, home free. The snow was a sort of unofficial welcoming committee. The whole experience was so surreal to them all they stood there until Paul and Duane woke them out of their reverie with piercing cries.

Gwen shook her head again at their naiveté. If only they knew, she thought.

China and Jean celebrated until they realized now that they had made something new; they had to live it out. The crying babies were good though because crying mouths had to be fed. Women had to be housed and there was work to be done. Without a word, the two turned and shared a private and knowing look. They had just needed a moment to soak it all in.

CHAPTER TWO

Gwen got a cab to stop. The short, dark-complexioned Italian man had all their bags in the trunk within thirty seconds. A seasoned hack, he didn't play with fares and he had worked out his own system where he could make three hundred a night. That didn't involve dawdling or hookers and he had worked out every step of a fare to mathematical precision. He looked admiringly at the women, gauging what to charge them.

The four of them, cramped into the back of his cab would have given him at least twelve dollars he thought, shaking his head, if it wasn't for the older chick who knew better. Gwen gave him instructions to drop them off on Fitch Boulevard and New York Boulevard. They got in the cab and on their way. The yellow checkered cab navigated its way from the airport across Conduit Boulevard, and then finally up New York Boulevard.

Jean surveyed the landscape of South Jamaica, Queens which was shortly to become his new home, sweet home. He observed all the bricks and concrete. No land, no animals, no air. There was too much everywhere, too much stuff built up, too many businesses, too many blue collar homes with their driveways and kept lawns. The atmosphere was gray and somber but the city was beautiful, where the snow covered it or met holiday lights.

They passed seedy looking tenement buildings which were sprinkled here and there along the boulevard, between the garbage and people that looked like things. There were a lot of people and Jean Paul studied them and the environment as they traveled. Some of them were very nice looking, some had faces that looked familiar and others looked so bad. "They are the Vietnam vets who just came home looking like that" Gwen says tisking. Even though his country was poorer, in Jamaica he'd never seen people that looked so bad, so sick that he turned involuntarily to Winsome to cover her eyes, not wanting her to see that hell.

She hadn't told him yet, anything to make him think her unhappy but he knew, she loved her mother and she'd had a very good life in the upper middle class neighborhood of Kingston Six, Jamaica, where she'd grown up. Since they'd first been together, she had gotten to see the other side of life. They'd made the best of it and their bond was strong but he felt a way about exposing her and his sons to hard times and danger. He hadn't known what to expect of Jamaica, Queens but he knew he would work hard and make a success of it no matter what. After all, when they'd first met, she was the don's girl.

She had been on the arm of Dexter Vassel, the son of Donovan Vassel, the warlord of West Kingston. Donovan had come up from a ragamuffin on the streets to controlling the whole area from Tivoli Gardens to Kingston Six and everything that happened in it. He was ruthless and powerful with numerous gangsters in his employ as well as a legion of scared people who cowered at even the mention of his name. He had the finest of everything and his reputation resounded near and far.

The father and the son were different though. The boy had grown up soft, used to having everything handed to him, and his every whim catered to. He'd never worked for what he had and his sense of entitlement made him abusive. He'd belittled Jean, an artist, for earning a living with his hands and that had spurred a rivalry that consumed Jean until he took Dexter's crown jewel, the beautiful Winsome. Jean had bested Dexter every time they went up against one another and their last confrontation had left Dexter with no doubts as to who was the victor.

They drove past a commercial strip of stores near 137th street Jean spotted Rosenberg Village to his right hand side. Jean almost gasped when he saw how huge the sprawling fifteen story twenty building brown brick co-op development was. No one with the exception of Gwen had ever seen that many buildings that stood so high in their lives. The neighborhood had changed and soon after they zoomed by the co-ops they came across a squat square of tall buildings, a "housing project" as Gwen called the Bedell Houses.

The projects were only on the other side of the street from where Gwen's apartment was on Fitch & New York Boulevard. Bedell Houses consisted of eight thirteen story buildings that somehow looked a tad bit more menacing then the area farther down the boulevard where the co-ops were. Jean studied the buildings of the complex that lay on both sides of New York Boulevard, as if he were dissecting them piece by piece. Reddish brown clay colored bricks held all the eight buildings of the complex together, where they had "window guards" on the windows. It must be like living in a prison to need bars on the window of your own home he said aloud as he surveyed the buildings.

Though everyone was in their own thoughts as they looked out the cab's windows, they all agreed. Jean could tell that in comparison to some of the houses he'd seen once he got near the projects, Fitch Boulevard was a poorer area than the rest of Queens that he'd seen thus far. And though he had seen every social class in his young twenty three years, it's like he had a built in radar for that type of thing, and could relate to all people who were poor and suffering throughout the globe. Indeed poverty is a language onto its self, and Jean could speak its many tongues and was well versed in understanding its many dialects.

Gwen instructed the driver to pull over in front of the house where she was renting an apartment. As the driver complied, she began to list some facts that she said she learned in the newspaper about where they were going to live. They got out of the car and with the men this time carrying the boys and Winsome and Gwen their few bags, they followed her into their brand new home at 170-10 Fitch Boulevard. Jean-Paul started walking in the lead in the general direction of the front door before Gwen had to stop him.

" Nah mon…gwaan over deh so!"

Gwen pointed toward the alley way on the right side of the house. The entrance to her basement apartment was on the side of the house. The house where Gwen lived was much like many of the homes in southeast Queens built toward the end of World War II. They were designed to be affordable for vets returning home from the war. People with city jobs, teachers, social workers and nurses and their spouses who worked in construction, carpentry, as electricians, drivers, in the hospital, and the airport, people who were considered the middle class populated these neighborhoods. The house was grey and white with a slanted black roof in the shape of the letter A. It also had a small lawn in front, with a driveway that led to the back of the house on its left side.

On their way in, Gwen told them more about the situation they'd be moving into. At the top floor of the three story home was a young nurse named Alice who had a five year old but wasn't with the father. Alice's daughter was adorable, a bright, happy girl named Shadele. The landlord, Mr. Humes, lived on the first two floors. He'd gotten the house through a veteran's program after serving in the Korean War. He worked as a manger in a big department store named Alexander's on 59th & Lexington in Manhattan. He kept his home neat and nicely decorated. Gwen thought he was rich. She told them collecting social security benefits was his main source of income, while the rents he collected from Gwen and Alice paid his mortgage.

Both women had their own door to their separate apartments, they just had to share the hallway and from time to time they would see one another in passing. From the mezzanine level of the stairs Gwen began to descend to open the door to her living quarters. And even though Gwen told everyone to watch their heads coming down the stairs, somehow China managed to scrape the top of his head on a slope that jutted down the stairs near Gwen's door. They teased him playfully and everyone finally got a chance to get a bird's eye view of their new living arrangement.

Gwen's place was small and neat more designed for efficiency than anything else. In the seven to eight years that Gwen had been living there she managed to transform that basement into her home. The place spoke volumes about her work ethic and ability to be self sufficient. Even though she sent a large portion of her income back to Jamaica every month to support her mother, she still did her best to make a good life for herself in New York too. The whole of the basement was at her disposal. There weren't any other walls used as dividers for separate rooms, just one big open space with the ceiling about seven feet from the floor. In the corners were the boiler room and a giant closet where Mr. Humes kept tools.

In Queens, even at that time, basement apartments were illegal because most of the time the hot water heater for the whole dwelling was in the basement. The toxic carbon monoxide fumes emitted from water heaters were deadly and had silently killed thousands throughout the city. There was also the high probability of flooding during storms and sometimes lack of ventilation, which made illnesses fester, and ways to escape in case of a fire. There had been times when untreated sewer water would flood basements and contaminate the whole lower half of a dwelling.

But because the rent for a basement apartment was half to a quarter what you would pay for a regular apartment, there was no shortage of potential tenants. Gwen could not care less about the legal issues of her apartment, as long as she had a decent place to rest her head. Gwen was an illegal alien with no green card, or legitimate working papers and she had to take what she could get. In many instances throughout the city, but especially in Queens, all that mattered to landlords was that you had your first month's rent, last, deposit and that the rent was on time.

Her dim apartment had brown shag carpeting on the floors and wooden paneling on the walls. Her furniture was heavily carved wood as well, secondhand but well cared for and her bed was neatly made in a homemade quilt. She had few decorations, a small heater, some jars of perfume on her dresser and clothing still in the dry cleaning bags hanging from a hook on one of the two big square columns. The carpet covered nearly the whole place except for where the stove and sink were in middle of the basement, about five feet away from the door leading to the small bathroom.

There was a small walk way between the stove, cabinets, and the lavatory. On the opposite side of the walk way, Gwen had made a little nook with a small dining table surrounded by four metal chairs with orange cushions. Above the table was the only window in the whole place. The window was small only about two feet tall and one foot wide but Gwen loved it because it let in the sunlight. It also boasted a grand panoramic view of the corner of Fitch & New York Boulevard, as well as the bottoms of the three project buildings that lay on that side of New York Boulevard. Her beautiful plants adorned the window and gave her small place charm.

Gwen's one luxury was the floor model black and white TV positioned in the center of the room. Atop the TV was a lace handkerchief under old black and white photos of the Stewart clan from years gone by. There was a picture of Gwen and Winsome who were five years apart as lasses holding hands both wearing pony tails. There were also other pictures of their father holding their mother Iceline in much happier times as well as others of their cousins and several other close loved ones. The pictures frames were good quality and it was easy to see the care she'd put into choosing them. Gwen was a firm believer in keeping a home that was spic and span. The small basement was immaculate and what she lacked in capitol she surely made up for with imagination. Although Gwen didn't have much, she was brought up to be a lady.

They put down the bags and Winsome and Jean sat on chairs while Gwen elected to sit on the edge of her bed. She invited China to come sit next to her by looking his way and patting a spot on her bed. The two couples started to decompress. Winsome and Jean were laughing and talking as they undressed the babies while Gwen was very attentive to Chinaman, gently massaging the area of his scalp that he'd injured, sensually running her fingers through his curly locks of black hair.

After settling down for a while, Gwen turned on the TV and gave them short introductions to the programs and characters. Gwen and Winsome took care of the babies and plotted what they would eat as it was too late to go to the market and get groceries, and she didn't have enough in the kitchen to feed everyone. Not to mention, as tired as she was from the flight, she could not stand up and cook anyway.

"Today, you get a special treat. You all get your first taste of pizza!" Gwen said.

"Pizza, how you mean pizza? We should just make what you have." Winsome stated striving to be considerate of their spending budget.

Gwen waved her away, dismissing the concern. "No Winnie…you're gonna like this here pizza. It's made by real Italians and it taste so good, you know. Besides, after being on the plane for so long, and all that we been through today, I don't feel like cooking tonight. We'll go food shopping tomorrow, and after that we can go shopping on Jamaica Avenue to get you all some clothes better fit for New York."

Winsome didn't need much more persuasion. An hour later, the girls returned from Napoli's pizzeria on Linden Boulevard with two boxes of large pies. They got out plates, gave out the slices and everyone dug in heartily. They thoroughly enjoyed their very first taste of American fast food.

The only problem they had with the pizza was getting used to the idea of eating with their hands. Jean seemed to love the pizza the most. He made orgasmic faces of approval for his meal as if he'd just taken a bite out of heaven. He was falling in love with America already.

They all sat making jokes, eating and laughing, blissfully enjoying their first night in America. When it was time for bed, Gwen and China put the twins to sleep. Winsome and Jean went to the bathroom so Jean could take a shower while Winsome brushed her hair. When they finally reemerged, China was fast asleep next to the boys. Gwen had finished setting up a fold out bed that she used to sleep in before Mr. Humes had blessed her with his dying mothers beautiful colonial bedroom set.

Seconds later, with their twins between them, they were sound asleep. Gwen woke Chinaman up and he went into the small bathroom for a shower. Later, as they all drifted off to sleep, bells sounded somewhere in the distance, striking midnight and according to the calendar, a new day. But for Winsome, Jean-Paul and China, it signified something much more important. It signified their first day in a foreign land.

Back in the Beverly Hills section of Kingston, Jamaica, things were on quite another note for Donovan Vassel. The dark, intense man dressed in a powder blue silk shirt and linen pants paced the floors of his palatial home, without expression. Methodically, back and forth he stalked the halls, which everyone around him knew meant he was at his most dangerous. He was like a panther; taut, waiting, coiled to strike. The first person to feel his wrath would end up dead or bloody. Though everyone wanted to ask him numerous questions and what the plan was after what had happened, no one dared approach him.

Donovan was grief stricken about the brutal slaying of his beloved son, his nephews and his most trusted and highest ranking soldiers. He'd gotten the news of their deaths more than an hour after they'd been ambushed in a restaurant and shot in the head while kneeling. His son had lived the life of a badman and he had no conclusive proof of who could have done it. There were too many people with too many reasons to even begin to know. But he had his suspicions.

His eyes were blood shot red, and the look of confusion and condemnation was bitterly engraved on his face like granite. The hardest pill for him to swallow was that he couldn't be sure whoever he ordered now to do the killings in retaliation wasn't one of the team that had killed them. Donovan couldn't trust anyone. It could have been anybody who hated him or Dexter personally, for any multitude of reasons.

Maybe it was the political factions that he represented. He thought to himself that possibly they'd somehow found out that he was playing both sides of the fence. Maybe it was some suppliers that he'd force to negotiate new terms after they'd given him the product. Maybe it was someone Dexter had robbed or extorted maybe it was Jean.

He couldn't be sure but knew by the manner in which it was done that it definitely was personal. He'd have his revenge but in the end, it wouldn't matter who killed them. His son, nephews, legal killer Bigga, and his utmost henchmen were all no more. The one consolation was that the night before, Dexter had had announced a wedding date for him and his girlfriend Pamela, who was now bearing his unborn child. Dexter would live on… in fragments.

Donovan's mind was perplexed as to who the culprit could have been that caused him so much grief in one fell swoop. His prejudice and shortsightedness would never allow him to believe Jean-Paul was actually capable of sending the slugs that burnt like hell fire through his son's cranium disintegrating it into pure oblivion. There wasn't enough of Dexter's head left on his shoulders to begin to think that an open casket funeral was even remotely plausible. Donovan's mind raced again and again through so many enemies in his mind whom he thought may have been responsible to retaliate against.

He'd put the order out to his second string goons to kill anybody on sight who they even thought had anything to do with his son's death. He roamed the halls of his home looking deranged, an unlit cigarette dangling from the left corner of his cotton dry mouth. He was clutching a blue steel 357 caliber magnum in his right hand and a tall glass of Scotch in his left hand. The only person he could bear was Stacy, Dexter's mother because she was not only unafraid of him despite his obvious imbalance; she was the only other person who shared this particular grief with him. Their normally tumultuous relationship helped him face the raw reality that his son was gone.

Ultimately, he knew in his heart, he was responsible for his son's demise. He'd tried to make his son into something he wasn't nor had to be and it cost him his existence in this realm. Donovan was one of the most powerful men in the whole Caribbean, and could have any woman, car, jewelry or whatever other material item he wanted at his beck and call. However, now, for all his power and influence- he could never bring his son back to life. The one thing he desired the most over all other things in his entire existence was the one thing he could never again have.

A parent isn't supposed to live a longer life than their children, and Donovan was experiencing a hurt like no other he'd ever imagined was possible. However, he still wasn't feeling one tenth of the pain and torment that he'd inflicted on so many families during his reign as a crime lord. Jean, who he knew could have never found the balls to pull a gun on Dexter, was only one of thousands that the Vassels had crossed over many years. Donovan paced the hall all night until the sun came up, and then pitifully, he made his way to his luxurious bedroom and lay out on the floor several feet from the massive wooden bed where Stacy lay, after whimpering for hours.

The same dawn of the morning's sun that illuminated the shores of the isle of Jamaica slowly rose over Jamaica, Queens as well. While the new horizon brought pain and confusion for the remaining members of the Vassel clan, it represented a new beginning as well as hope and the promise for prosperity in a new land for Jean and the others. Everyone except for Winsome gradually started rising out of their slumber at about eight that morning. Winsome had gotten up about an hour and a half before everyone else because the twins started crying. When she awoke, it had taken her a minute to focus and remember where she was and then to study the little basement in the new morning light. Then, as nimbly as she could to not wake Jean, she'd nursed the boys.

Now, one by one everyone started to take turns filing into Gwen's small, but neat bath room to freshen up and prepare for their first official day as New Yorkers. After everything was said and done it took everyone about two and half hours to get ready and be prepared to walk out the door. Gwen called a taxi and she, Jean and China were dropped off on Jamaica Avenue & 165th street, in the heart of Jamaica's commercial shopping district. They ran into the first store selling coats, scurrying to get out of the thirty degree frost that Winsome and the babies had dared not brave, and bought the warmest coats, gloves, and wool hats they could find for her, themselves and the babies. They paid for their new wears and, and in fact wore them right out of the store.

Afterwards they went gallivanting through the shopping district on Jamaica Avenue. All newcomers to the country are in absolute awe and astonishment of all the lights and modernity of their new found home. However due to the season, there were also Christmas decorations and lighting gracing Jamaica Avenue and it was not only festive but beautiful. True they had also celebrated this time of the year in the Caribbean; however it was not quite in the same fashion as it seemed to be in New York.

Everyone walked fast, talked fast, drove fast and they found it hard to believe how extremely fast paced everything, and everyone seemed to be moving. To them it was an extraordinary pace, but Gwen had grown accustomed to it in all her years of living in New York. It just seemed odd to the others because it seemed if as everyone was in such a rush, to go nowhere fast. There were people shouting at one another and cars honking their horns maneuvering around each other at break neck speeds, only to stop at a traffic light at the end of the block.

It wasn't lost on many of the natives that Jean and the others were out -of- towners either. They could easily tell by how slow they moved and the loud colors they wore, as well as the deeply accented patois they spoke. In several stores, when Jean asked if they could be helped, they had to be asked to repeat themselves several times before the clerk could understand what they were saying. At first it bothered him, but then he just chalked it up to part of the adjustment to their new environment. They all had a good laugh about how ironic it was that they ended up in America living in a place called Jamaica yet people had a hard time understanding them speak.

"Fuck 'appen' fi dem… deh…dey nah speak English or something?" China joked.

They took in the sights on Jamaica Ave., and shopped about three hours soaking up their new environment before returning to Gwen's Fitch Boulevard flat. By the time they were done, they were loaded down with winter garments for everyone as well as several thick comforters and quilts. For Gwen was allowing everyone to stay at her flat until they all had enough money to get on their feet, China had gone ahead of them in line and bought her a jazzy silk navy blue blouse she'd been eyeballing. Her face lit up with the glee of a child, brighter than the Christmas decorations that adorned Jamaica Avenue with appreciation.

China had also brought supplies for the house and several outfits for his God-children. They had fun holding the new clothes up on the twins and unpacking all the new things. After everyone had gotten settled in, Winsome and Gwen went grocery shopping at the local super market a few blocks away on New York Boulevard. As they walked down the boulevard back and forth to the grocery store they surveyed their new neighborhood. Winsome carefully noting markers in case she ever found herself lost.

The next day was Saturday, and Gwen took every one to Manhattan to see all the sights that there were to see from the Empire State Building, to Times Square, and the Brooklyn Bridge. Everyone was overwhelmed with joy, because not only were they taking in the sights but making their stakes as bonafide New Yorkers. It was a dream come true for all of them, and if like Gwen said there were so many jobs available, and opportunities for the prospect of advancement, that was just mind blowing to Jean. He figured that if he can come to Jamaica and, make it without knowing anybody then coming to New York would definitely be a piece of cake with his family. He could feel it in his bones; it would be easy.

After all… he'd just gotten away with murder scot free and his opposition had been among the absolute best Jamaica had to offer. What could any one of these Yankee boys do to him that hadn't already been done? He asked himself, grinning widely. Oh yeah New York looked like a giant chocolate cake with a big fat juicy cherry on top of it. At least that's Jean thought to himself as he overlooked the city, ninety stories high up in the air above the ground on the observation deck of the Empire state building.

CHAPTER THREE

Their first weekend in New York came and went in a flash. Monday came too fast and it was time for Gwen to return to work. She worked as a maid for The Silvermans, a rich white family with an eight bed room mansion in Dix Hills, out in Long Island. Gwen had been living with a very dear and old friend of her mother whom she'd grown up with in Jamaica and that they considered to be an aunt. The older woman's name was Mrs. Willcott. However, once she responded to an ad in the paper for domestic help and got the job with the Silvermans, she had moved on. The new position enabled her to afford her keep and her own apartment.

Mr. Silverman was a big shot lawyer who worked in a sky high building in Manhattan, Gwen told them. The white man was short and pudgy and couldn't come to terms with his male pattern baldness. He still tried to comb the hair from the sides of his head over the bald spot at the top. His wife Tanya was a blonde haired white woman who at forty five, was ten years his junior. She was also a bit taller than him, about five eight, five nine.

Even though she was now middle aged, she still obsessed over her figure and talked fondly about years gone by when she was a model, and a Miss New York. She was a socialite, something Gwen couldn't explain to the three Caribbean born and bred foreigners who had never heard of such a thing. She also served as a hostess for her husband Ira's numerous functions. They had four children.

Tanya was a very loving and endearing mother; however the ins and outs of domestic life just weren't for her…that's where Gwen came into the picture. All Tanya wanted to do was shop and gossip with her rich friends on the phone, and in person. Her whole life was a series of dresses and parties and she couldn't be bothered to wash a dish or sweep a floor. Not that Gwen minded Tanya was the reason Gwen had solid work while many other maids had to take three and four assignments a week, never knowing how long they would last.

Tanya's lack of domestic skills and her love of Gwen's Long Island Ice Teas, and Bloody Marys were a blessing. She drank one after another most afternoons while she waited for her husband to arrive home. Afterwards, she'd get all dolled up in the new clothes she'd bought and go out to different functions in the evenings. The Silvermans attended at least three functions a week the whole seven and a half years Gwen worked for them.

They paid Gwen excellently – more than $150.00 a week, off the books. In those days no one paid household help as employees or thought to offer benefits such as insurance. It was come and go job and most employers paid poorly, knowing most maids were illegals or desperate mothers and no one would advocate on their behalf. Gwen was blessed with the job at the Silvermans and her excellent performance as well as discretion made them feel more than glad to have her. Mr. Silverman knew his wife had a drinking and spending problem but the few times when he'd tried to ask Gwen about it, Gwen had refused to be part of it in any way. She also knew, he realized certain things about him, from receipts in his pockets and lipstick on his collar, that she'd never breathed a word to Mrs. Silverman about.

On work days, Gwen normally got up around five A.M. She'd catch the Long Island Rail Road's 6:15 express train headed east to Dix Hills. She'd normally meet the family's driver at the station at about a quarter to seven. There was no public transportation in the exclusive neighborhoods and the Silverman's beautiful house on the hills would have taken more than an hour to walk to. Mr. Ira, as she called him, had arranged transport from the station for Gwen so her not having a car wouldn't be an obstacle. She arrived a little before seven everyday and made breakfast for the Silverman children before the driver dropped them off behind the gates of their private schools.

She cleaned the house in sections, starting from the den in the Northeastern corner and working her way out. That morning, just as the children left, Gwen overheard Mr. Silverman angrily complaining to someone on the phone in the study about how he couldn't wait to get to his office so he could fire his lush of a janitor. Whoever Mr. Silverman was talking to on the other end had to endure an almost ten minute tirade about how the janitor left his office in shambles every Friday, had failed to sweep and vacuum and how he always smelled of liquor, and was so wasted by the time he got there that he never did his job properly.

Seeing a platinum opportunity present itself right in front of her face, Gwen quickly capitalized on the moment and asked to speak to the angry crimsoned faced man as soon as he hung up the phone.

"Mr. Ira may I have a word with you for a moment?" Gwen cautiously probed.

"Sure Gwen, what is it?" He shot back, picking up his briefcase and blazer. As soon as the driver returned he would be taken to the Long Island Railroad station. The anger was still registered on his face but he took care to change his tone, to not offend Gwen.

"I'm sorry, but I couldn't help but overhear that you are going to fire the cleaning person at your office... I-" But before Gwen could finish her statement Ira cut her off.

"Listen Gwen, you're a good kid and a very hard worker, that's why I need you here with my family. I know that I can trust you to get the job done, whatever it might be.
I could never possibly afford to lose you to work in the office. I pay a mint in rent for that suite and I know you can make it look worth every dime but this home is more important to me. So what do you say to a little extra in your Christmas bonus this year to make sure you're happy, huh?"

Gwen appreciated the compliment and she was certainly looking forward to the bonus. The Dix Hills winter made Queens seem like spring time and she did work hard keeping the gigantic home immaculate but she had another hustle in mind. "Oh no…that's not what I was going to say. It just that I heard you talking about that wretched man there so and my sister is here, and looking for work. She would do a very good job and I highly recommend her. Very bright girl, honest and hard working. I was going to ask if you could use my sister to fill the position you were just speaking of."

Silverman didn't have to think about it twice. "Any sister of yours is always welcome to work for me. I know if she's half as good as you I'll be a thousand times better off than with the turkey I have now. I feel sorry for him because he has a big family and I kept looking away and letting things slide but no more. I'm going to let this man give me one last day's work, and then I'm gonna fire him at the end of his shift. That's more than fair. Your sister can start tomorrow at nine in the morning. I'll pay her the same rate I paid Juan, the same $125.00 a week. I'll give you the instructions to my office tonight when I come home from work."

Gwen was ecstatic and she knew Winsome would be too. "Thank you Mr. Ira! She won't let you down and she'll be there tomorrow with bells on!" She clapped him on the shoulder and though he didn't show it, he marveled at the young Black woman's strength. "Oh and by the way… thanks for the extra bonus too, hear."

Owens, the driver, beeped the horn outside and the two of them both laughed as he made his way to the door. There Gwen waved goodbye happily, patting herself on the back for the sly way she made Mr. Silverman commit to giving her a little extra in her Christmas bonus that year.

The day zoomed by and six thirty rolled around and so did Mr. Silverman out of his black and silver Mercedes sedan with Owens at the wheel. Just as he promised once he got himself together he gave Gwen the instructions to his office, and told her to have her sister meet him there at nine A.M. sharp. Gwen stashed them in her purse as she walked out the door waving good night to Tanya and the kids on her way to the Long Island Rail Road Station. Now that Winsome was for all intents and purposes employed at Mr. Silverman's office, she thought to herself one down…two to go in regard to the rest of her extended family members obtaining employment.

She couldn't wait to get home and tell everyone the excellent news she had. When she got home and shared the news with everyone, the whole apartment erupted in cheers. Gwen was so happy about Winsome getting the job she almost forgot that they were supposed to formally start the nine night celebration in memory of their beloved slain mother. When they'd left Jamaica things had been so hectic that they never got a chance.

She covered the table with a white cloth, on which fried fish and white bread occupied center stage. They sang hymns until midnight when superstition says the spirit of the deceased passes through and has something to eat. Then with blessings and tearful remembrances, they lit a candle and consigned her memory. Even though, the mood became somewhat somber once they started celebrating the memory of their mother, Jean spoke to remind them they weren't celebrating her death, but her life, their new life and all that still awaited all of them.

The next morning was hectic. Before Gwen left, she had to help Winnie memorize directions to the city, and prepare bottles for the two young babies. Winsome would have liked to stay at the apartment so she could nurse the twins a little longer but she knew finding a job her first week in America was a golden opportunity that she couldn't pass up.

Jean saw the job as a blessing, and an indicator of how easy it would be for him to get a job. He figured if his woman could get a job that quick then he was surely a shoe in for a job within the first two weeks of him being in New York. He calmed her nervous fears and got her so hyped about her good fortune that she practically marched to Silverman's office. She braved the Q113 bus to the E train and got off at 47th street and Seventh Ave. in Manhattan. Then she walked to 52nd street and rendezvoused with Mr. Silverman and with very little training or direction, began working.

CHAPTER FOUR

The seasons changed and the two weeks that Jean thought it would take for him to get a job had now turned to six months. Winsome and Gwen went to work while Jean and Chinaman still looked for employment. The two responded to ads in the papers and help wanted signs in windows but didn't have any luck. Jean would drop the twins off at Mrs. Willcott's house on Linden Boulevard, six blocks away from their home on Fitch while he and China did their fruitless job search. She tried to be very encouraging but day after day as Mrs. Willcott saw their frustrated faces when they returned.

Jean was starting to be very uncomfortable with being in Gwen's small flat. Both he and China were at the end of their savings. They weren't totally naive and they'd known things may get a little rough for them, but New York was proving unbelievably expensive and having the twins didn't make Jean's job any easier. Though both Jean and China found odd jobs here and there, the wages were hardly enough to support his whole family.

Before he had children he could sacrifice little things here and there and still be comfortable but there was no way to sacrifice pampers and milk. He had to provide at least twelve meals a day for him and his family for at least the next eighteen years. Even though, everyone pooled their resources together, Jean's pride and sense of independence made it harder and harder for him to bear it as the days wore on.   Since Gwen didn't have to send money home to her mother, the extra money went to her own household instead.

She said she didn't mind doing things she did but it didn't sit too well with Jean because he wasn't accustomed to being taken care of. He had been a leader and a bread winner for his family almost his entire life. Now that he was here in America, he couldn't find suitable employment; he couldn't maintain his own household and family. The prospects were dim because he wasn't a citizen nor did he have a green card and the same went for Chinaman as well. It embarrassed them that people would give women with no credentials a job, but not them. They were beginning to think that it was methodical, done intentionally to undermine their authority in the household, and to emasculate them as men in the eyes of the opposite sex.

What made matters even worse and added insult to injury is that some of the black Americans at the places they would apply for jobs would mock them and laugh directly in their faces. They had many confrontations because of people telling them to go back to their country on the same banana boat they came to America on or acting as if they were trying to take something of theirs rather than do an honest day's work. For the life of him, Jean couldn't understand why his own people in America would mock him and China. After all, it had only been a few years since the civil rights era and all the Jim Crow laws of the south had been abolished. People such as Malcolm X had preached the gospel of black unity on these same streets and Jean couldn't understand how these people who looked just like him could be so determined to ostracize and scapegoat him. The racism of his own people compounded his problems and weighed heavily on his mind.

Jean vowed to keep pushing on and persevere but Chinaman had started drinking. They had both decided that it was better to drink because the reefer they could get their hands on was nothing in comparison to the high grade herb they could get back home. They tried some ganja some of the new brethren they'd met had but all it seemed to do was give them a headache. Puffing ganja therefore wasn't a viable option for either one of the two best friends and they had decided drinking was the way to go instead. At first, China would take a small portion from the wages he earned from whatever odd jobs he and Jean did here and there and purchase a little bottle of liquor every so often. Jean would also partake in the libations with China from time to time but China soon needed to drink every day. He quickly reached the point where he couldn't meet dusk without a bottle.

In mid July of 1973, just when things seemed to be at their bleakest, they answered an ad in Newsday for landscapers and they both got the job. Their new gig paid only two dollars an hour plus whatever tips they earned. It was hard work but they took it and worked the long thirteen hour days from seven in the morning until eight in the evening or whenever the scorching unrelenting summer sun would set. Both men were indeed from a tropical climate however, the heat in New York was a different type of hot. Back home, they at least had the breeze off the sea to cool them, but the humid summer heat of New York was absorbed and reflected in all its concrete avenues and boulevards.

Working was hard on his body but good for Jean's mind and spirit. He was now able to put food on the table for the family. The summer came and went. Jean realized one morning that it was now September and the men only had another month or so to work until the ground froze and it was winter again. He was engrossed in this thought as he gathered some dirty clothes so he could take them to the laundry mat. He emptied the pockets of a pair of dungarees he hadn't worn the whole while he'd been in New York.

He came across a small piece of paper with a phone number on it and the name above the number read Judge Blackwell N.Y.C. At first Jean almost threw the piece of paper away until he remembered who Judge Blackwell was. Gwen didn't have a house phone in the small basement so he went to the corner and called. He thought of the short balding man whom he met back in Kingston while he was peddling his goods about two years before. Judge Blackwell and his lady friend had paid two hundred dollars for two beautiful paintings he sold them on the beach. Jean hadn't made anything in a long while, he realized wistfully.

The phone rang and much to his surprise and delight someone picked up on the other end after about four times.

"Hello…this is Larry." A business-like voice said on the other end of the phone.

Jean explained just exactly who he was and asked to speak to Judge Blackwell.

There was a pause and then a booming laugh. "Ah yes, Jean! My artist friend! Jean, do you know how many compliments I have gotten on those paintings? They are the centerpiece of my collection, young man. I have a Modigliani on one wall and yours on another and invariably, every night I'm asked, 'how much will you sell that to me for Judge?' and they are never talking about the Modigliani I paid three thousand for!"

He laughed heartily. "Jean, I am going to sell those paintings for ten thousand a piece one day, you mark my words! How are you, my friend?"

These words were like ice water to a man dying of thirst in the desert. Jeans spirits were lifted and he found himself smiling uncontrollably, his chest swelled. He filled the judge in on his exploits leaving out the parts of the story the judge didn't need to know. When he told the judge about his present employment, the older man gasped.

"Boy, you'll be in your grave at an early age working like that." The judge sighed.

Jean told him about his wife and twin sons and how much harder life had been before he was breaking his back as a landscaper and the older man paused.

"Son, you're right. You can't go back to having the whole weight on your lady but I don't agree with you working like a dog either. Listen, I know people and there's got to be something I can do. Let me do some digging and meet me next Monday here at the court. I can't promise anything because of the situation being what it is but I gave you my word and I'm glad that you thought of me." Stated judge Blackwell flatly.

Jean was elated after hearing the good news from the judge. Now he could work half the week at his landscaping job, collect some pay from there then go see what opportunity the judge was able to ferret out for him. All of Jean's despair, and anxieties were now slowly transforming themselves into his normal optimistic outlook on things. When Jean hung up the phone he was smiling from ear to ear and began telling every one of his new fortune and good news. China found that to be enough excuse for him and Jean to get a drink.

Even though it was Sunday and all the liquor stores were closed, that didn't stop China from getting what he wanted, and thought that he needed. China had become accustomed enough to the surroundings in his neighborhood to know that there was a spot that sold bootleg liquor on Sunday's by Mrs. Willcott's block. The going rate for any bootleg bottle of liquor was the original price plus half its cost. China loved his Jamaican rum. A large bottle was only $4.00 so at the bootlegger he'd have to pay six. He didn't mind the extra tax. The booze helped keep his mind off his troubles and it also reminded him of home.

Jean finished packing all the dirty clothes he was going to be washing into a metal cart with wheels on it to haul his clothes to the laundry mat and the two men made their way to the bootlegger where they bought some wine in addition to China's rum. They drank heartily as they washed their clothes. Jean was ecstatic and didn't notice that though Chinaman still laughed and cracked jokes as they talked shit to one another on the boulevard, he had lost the light in his eyes.

The judge had told him to meet him at the Queens County Court House where he was a judge in the appellate division that Monday at 8:00 A.M. sharp. It only took Jean a little while to find his courtroom downstairs in A.P. 2. The judge still looked exactly the same. He hadn't aged a second in the two years. He was as serious as a heart attack on the bench as Jean waited to speak with him and the young man felt intimidated momentarily.

But when he saw Jean as the courtroom emptied, he recognized him instantly. Jean met the judge at the door to his chambers and the old man grabbed him and hugged him heartily. He took Jean on a tour of the court, and introduced him to all of the court clerks and stenographers, most of whom were white women who had worked in the courts for decades. Normally, the building was a bastion of racism and injustice for the Blackman but because the judge thought so highly of Jean, the underlings practically bowed before him.

In chambers later, the judge explained to him how intensely competitive and guarded jobs at the courts were. Though he worked in the system, he had no delusions and he pulled no punches as he explained a little something about railroading and the profitability of prisons. Jean listened and learned, filled with respect that the judge dared speak his mind even in such a place. Assistant positions were usually reserved for undergrads from the best undergrad schools.

They began their law careers working as interns. The primarily Jewish law students who clerked in the courts before they were accepted to the bar were highly competitive and Jean's presence would not go unnoticed but Judge Blackwell had figured a way to get him in. Jean would be put on his personal payroll with no official title. He would do much the same things as a personal assistant, which actually was a glorified name for a "go-fer". The money wasn't great but Jean wasn't one to look a gift horse in the mouth and he gladly took the position. They talked more about cases and what the judge had going on and he told him the ins and outs of the Queens County Court House and the appellate division downstairs in A.P. 2 which is where he'd be based.

Jean worked a few more days with his landscaping job then started at the court with Judge Blackwell. Jean's duties varied daily depending on what the judge instructed him to do. Normally he would go get coffee for the judge and run documents from one part of the court house to another section of the court house all day. His job wasn't all that hard, and to Jean it was easy money. The judge frequently ran ideas past him, and listened to his opinions even though he never let on to what extent he used those opinions in formulating his rulings. Jean didn't mind working in the court house one bit and in fact really came to love it.

He started creating art again, painting and sculpting fine pieces that he sold at local flea markets on the weekends. Prior to him finding steady work, Jean just didn't have the same desire to create any artwork as he did back in the Caribbean. The need to provide for his family and the depression at not being able to do so first had a lot to do with him finding the proper outlets for his creations. Now that he secured a job he had a new lease on life and it gave him the inspiration to once again create his art.

Creating his artwork was a stress reliever for Jean; a true labor of love. Winsome would accompany Jean with the twins on the weekend to the flea market. After all they both worked full time and the family rarely had an opportunity to spend any quality time together. With both of their off the book incomes and now the money Jean made selling his work, they were doing fairly well for a young family new to this country.

About three months after Jean started working for the judge, they had enough money to move into a two bedroom flat. Mr. Humes had a family member down the block on Fitch that rented them a legal attic apartment. The new apartment surely wasn't the greatest, but at least they would have more space and privacy than they did at Gwen's. Jean shared a room with Winsome while China would sleep on the couch in the living room and the twins had their own bedroom as well.

Things were finally starting to go pretty smooth for them a year after arriving in New York. Especially considering they only knew about three people put together between them before they moved to the States. Their only major obstacles now were to get China a job, and also obtain their green cards and citizenship so they too could get better work. Even though China didn't have a steady job, he was still able to be very creative and resourceful with what he'd earn working several odd jobs.

He shined shoes part time at the Long Island Railroad station on Sutton Boulevard. He also got himself an early morning paper route servicing his immediate area in South Jamaica. To most those jobs were menial labor, but China didn't care. He had to take what he could get, at least for the time being. The pay wasn't the greatest however it at least allowed him to have some money in his pockets every week.

Jean and Winsome didn't charge China any money for rent. They just wanted him to save his money so he could get on his feet and be independent. China was far from a bum or freeloader. Even though he wasn't paying any rent he made it his business and duty to keep the whole house spotless. Especially the kitchen, bathroom, and the living room area near the couch where he slept.

He knew Winsome was in Manhattan cleaning offices all day and it didn't make sense for him to be living there rent free and for her to have to come home and clean after a ten hour day which included her commute to and from work. Winsome still had to come home and tend to her man and children. He figured that everyone already had enough headaches and this was his way of helping out. Not that they minded his being there, both of them were more than mere friends, they were his family and the twins loved him.

December rolled around and it was their one year anniversary in America. To celebrate, the whole family including Gwen got together. With Winsome working so much and taking care of the twins when she got home from her ten hour days, she rarely got a chance to even see Gwen anymore. Gwen had gotten a house phone and she and Winsome would speak to one another on the phone almost every day to see if everything was fine or not...especially after the brutal slaying of their beloved mother. If they were lucky, they would actually see one another only once or twice a week.

Winsome noticed Gwen had an extremely hard time getting up the stairs to their attic apartment. She really didn't think too much of it at first, but then she also noticed that Gwen was wearing clothes a little baggier than usual. She also noticed how frequently her big sister had to run to the bathroom in the two hours that had passed since she'd been there. It seemed as if she was excusing herself to use the bathroom every ten minutes or so. In Winsome's heart of heart's she knew something wasn't totally kosher with the strange things she observed about Gwen and the way she was behaving. In a flash, she knew what the matter was. While Jean and China listened to Frankie Crocker on the radio and played dominos in the living room, she playfully confronted her in the kitchen.

"So what a gwaan…is everything alright with you, must we rush you to the doctor's office immediately?" Winsome pretended to lift Gwen who pushed her away like she was such a fool.

"No…no I'm alright, perfectly fine. Why do you ask? Do I look like I need to go to the doctor?" Gwen tried to act normal but she looked green around the gills even as she spoke.

"Listen…we nah rich as yet, but mi and Jean have a little money saved up for emergencies, and if you need fi go see the doctor then let me know. You is mi sister and mi only family now, and if you need help ,I'll be more than glad to help after how much you helped the whole ah we here in foreign…you see me?" Winsome stated quite earnestly.

Gwen laughed and swatted her away again. "Ounoo need fi save the doctor money seen…I don't need no money fi a doctor mi need you fi take the money and throw me a baby shower instead!"

Winsome was speechless for a second and then she hugged Gwen. She felt like a putz for not noticing that Gwen was already showing. She thought back to their conversations about what could only have been her having morning sickness. Gwen stood up from the bed where she was sitting and revealed the whole mystery to Winsome. She was six months pregnant, and China was the father of her soon to be first born. Winsome was ecstatic when she heard the news. She would be an aunt and that the twins would have a new little cousin to grow up with in the New York. Now that Gwen had given Winsome her good news the meaning of their celebration was elevated to a whole other level. They went back into the living room where Mrs. Willcott, Jean, China, and the now fourteen month old twins were to make the announcement to everybody.

"Gwen is going to be a mommy everybody!"

Winsome burst out with glee as soon as the two sisters walked back into the living room. Every one gave the announcement a round of applause. They were all happy to hear about the new addition to the family. China stood up from the table where he and Jean were playing dominos and made his way over to Gwen and put his arm around her. Once he did that there was no question in anyone's mind as to who the father could be.

Even though Jean and China were close, and trusted one another with the others life, China never told Jean he was romantically involved with Gwen. It didn't matter to Jean. Gwen being pregnant with China's seed was no big surprise to him. He knew that back home in Jamaica, China was a ladies' man. China had told him one time that he'd had a crush on Gwen when they were younger. He should have seen the signs and how touchy feely they were since they were on the plane sitting together on the way to New York.

In all reality, China and Gwen's relationship was born out of sheer convenience. She worked such long hours and had no time to pursue men. She didn't trust the strangers that tried to come on to her in the street and she didn't feel any attraction for them. China always did hold a torch for Gwen and when she started coming on to him he just did what came natural.

The two had been intimate since the first week China was in the States. Whenever Jean and Winsome would leave for a half an hour or more, China and Gwen would have hot and wild romps all throughout Gwen's apartment. And once China moved in with Jean and Winsome, he'd stop by Gwen's house down the street after they both got off from work and they'd get each other off with no interruptions.

Jean was already raising his twins to respect China as their uncle, and now by him and Gwen having a child together that made it that much more official. In fact, China and Gwen had plans on announcing the news to everyone that evening. Winsome's worries about her sister forced the announcement just a trifle bit prematurely. There was still another announcement to make that evening.

Holding a glass of wine in one hand and his arm around Gwen with the other, China announced, "Gwen and I are also going to be living together. John, you and Winnie are my family and have been very nice to me, but now I'm going to give you two your space so I can be closer to the mother of my child."

He was grinning from ear to ear, causing his slanted eyes to seem even smaller as he made the announcement. It was also a great relief and a load off both Gwen and China's shoulders to make that announcement because now they didn't have to sneak around to be with each other anymore.

CHAPTER FIVE

Ten years had passed since that night China and Gwen made the announcement that she was going to be having his baby. The year now was 1983 and much had changed since they first arrived in the States. Always striving to do better for himself, Jean convinced Judge Blackwell to be his sponsor in a program that allowed court employees to enroll in the Queens County paralegal course. He was not technically an employee of the courts but Judge Blackwell vouched for Jean and pulled a couple of strings.

Jean became a naturalized citizen. He then legally married Winsome at the court house which made her and the twins U.S. Citizens. He took the six month course and became a paralegal for the city court system of New York. Now that he was a paralegal his salary changed dramatically. Between him working in the court system and selling his art on the weekends, he was able to bring in a little over twenty five thousand a year after everything was said and done.

Winsome also had a change of fortune for the better since they all became citizens in 1978. She made strides to get better work as well. She enrolled in York College which was only about three miles from where they lived on Fitch Boulevard, and followed her neighbor Alice's advice and took up classes in nursing.

In 1979, after almost two years of taking part time classes after work, Winsome graduated from the program and became a licensed practical nurse. Alice recommended her to one of her supervisors and got her a job working with her at Miriam Immaculate Hospital right off 150th street and Jamaica Avenue.

Even though the hours she worked seemed to be nonstop around the clock, the money was very good because of all the overtime it required. Winsome was able to quit the cleaning job in Manhattan and work full time at the hospital. She liked working close to her home instead of trifling with the super crowded E and F trains to and from the city.

Her new job was only about three miles away from her door and only required she ride one bus. Winsome was also making a good salary now. It had been a very slow paced grind for them to have made it to the point they were now. Success was finally arriving. With Winsome and Jean being legal citizens and having legitimate incomes, they were able to get a first time homeowners loan. They purchased a two family home in the Saint Albans section of Jamaica.

In all, the house cost a little less than $100,000.00 which was an arm and a leg at the time. However, the potential income and help with the mortgage the attic apartment would provide made the house irresistible to both Jean and Winsome. Besides they had a whole thirty years to pay the mortgage off, and they didn't plan on leaving any time soon. They felt it was important to leave something to their children. The house was a valuable asset that could stay in the family for generations to come. It took them ten years but they'd planted a strong foundation in America and were damned proud of themselves.

China and Gwen had also moved up in the world. As a result of Jean becoming a citizen, he was able to get Judge Blackwell to pull a few strings for China as well. One of the Judge's colleagues from law school had married China and Gwen and they too became U.S. citizens. After China became a citizen he made his steaks by driving cabs, and also kept his most lucrative paper route in Jamaica Queens. In the mornings he made his paper drops from the yellow checkered N.Y.C. cab he was renting to own.

After he paid for his cab and the medallion that registered it with the city he was able to pull in about $25,000.00 a year. Once he paid the cab off, he'd probably be able to pull in an additional $10,000.00 a year. Gwen still was working for the Silverman's, but since their children were all pretty much adults, her hours weren't as long anymore. Now she worked from the hours of 7 A.M. to 3:00 P.M. which allowed her time to come home and attend to her own family.

Since China was making more money now and the family was stable, he followed Jean and Winsome's cue and also took the necessary steps to buy a home for his family. The only thing China didn't have was the luxury of Gwen earning as much as Winsome did and her income was still off the books. China went to the same bank and loan officer as Jean did and was able to get a loan for $80,000.00. He used his taxi as collateral for the loan. He still had two years left to pay on the cab before he owned it and the worth of the cab was far less than the worth of the loan.

However, China flashed $25,000.00 that represented his family's life savings and that motivated the loan officer to shuffle a few papers and call in China's loan as a favor when he saw how serious they were about buying a house. Besides he'd done good business with Jean and was on a roll. The next business week, Mr. and Mrs. Peter Chin used the loan to buy a house that was still in the South Jamaica vicinity on Fitch and Rockaway Boulevard. It was just across Bedell Park Pond about six blocks away from where they'd lived by the projects. It was a white two story home with a basement and three bedrooms.

They also took the thirty year payment plan. They ended up renting the basement to a dark skinned Trinidadian fellow named Godfrey. The only set back to that was that they'd have to still go to the Laundry mat instead of washing their clothes down stairs. However with two pre-teens in the house, they needed all the money they could get.

China couldn't help but to laugh to himself. He'd come full circle, from shacking up with Gwen eleven years earlier. Also working odd jobs for five whole years before he could find steady work on two jobs to now having two children and owning his own home and being able to rent space to one of his fellow West Indians. The whole thing just tickled him pink. He thought of how many times he just wanted to go home after he'd been ridiculed for just striving to provide for his growing family. Now all of his family's hard work was paying off. Now, for all the times he had been called a banana boat boy, he was able to laugh the loudest as he moved into his new home.

And whereas he, Jean and their families had been the only other West Indian people he knew, there was now a flourishing community of others who had come in the late seventies and established themselves. These people were dotted in the owners and renters of the houses in their Southside neighborhood. They were heavily concentrated in Queens Village and Cambria

Heights sections of Jamaica and other parts of Queens as well as the Flatbush area in Brooklyn.

They were still outnumbered by the native Blacks who had been here and as a protective measure many of them pooled their resources to buy businesses, learn trades and invest in real estate. For the most part they didn't mingle with the Black Americans and sent their children to private schools, music lessons and to learn ballet. They were still an isolated community but they managed to carve out their own identity. They had their own parties and fashion and spoke patois with ease around the Americans. The adults such as Jean and Chinaman could kick back now and they were living a decent life.

However, things weren't always so rosy for any of their children at school. Unlike most West Indians they didn't choose to put their children in private school and as neither of them were religious enough, to subject them to the Catholics either. They wanted their children to get the basics and make their own way without getting caught up in the decay around them. The neighborhood was blue collar, working class but the shadow of the projects loomed large.

There was a constant threat of violence and crime had to be at the forefront of your mind. The violence filtered down to the youth and school was a wild place instead of the strict hall of learning they'd known in their schooling. China and Gwen's children P.J. and Dorrine were stair steps at ages nine and ten. China had named his son Peter as well so everyone called Jean's son Peter by his middle name, Duane.

China's son Peter was called P.J., short for Peter Junior to distinguish the two apart. They were only about a year and a half apart in age but Duane and his cousin P.J. were running partners from day one. Paul followed in their footsteps, even though he was technically the same age as Peter. The kids attended the schools that were near Fitch and New York Boulevard. The twins were now eleven in the sixth grade and attended I.S. 72 on New York Boulevard about a mile south of where they used to live on Fitch Boulevard. They looked exactly alike and had grown to be rather handsome young boys. They had their mother's curly locks of hair all jet black, her almond shaped eyes and nose, but their father's exact dark mahogany completion.

Jean got the greatest joy there was watching them grow into young men. When they were young they looked just like their mother, however the more they matured the more they looked and acted more like Jean every day though in different ways. They were identical physically but you could tell the twins apart by their attitudes; they were the exact extreme polar opposites. Paul was the docile class clown type while Duane was extremely bright yet belligerent, and at a drop of a dime he was ready to rumble!

At this time their parents were still dressing them alike. They'd pretty much have the same outfits in different colors. That combined with their slight accent and odd pronunciation of their last name made them a target for middle school bullies. They twins had lived in Queens all but a couple of months of their lives yet still had a very slight hint of a Caribbean accent because of their parent's deep accents. Not to mention that all four children were teased because their sir names were very unusual for black people.

Baptiste and Chin were not commonplace names in their school and the prejudice against West Indians Jean had first battled in the seventies had only worsened. There was a Republican president in the White House and he appealed to his base by egging on their most racist and anti poor hatred. He had created a fictional character called the "Welfare Queen" to stereotype all Black American women. The Black Americans in turn misunderstood the new West Indians culture which caused a divide in the community. Ultimately both sides of the divide were being used as tools and slaves to the system being made to think that they were all different.

The immigrants looked down on the Black Americans because they believed the stereotypes they'd learned about them from the media. Behind closed doors, they saw them as Welfare Queens and brutal, savage animals who loved to fight for no reason and horrendous parents. This prejudice filtered down to the kids and they all got a taste of it as well. Poor little P.J. though got it the worst though.

The kids would make fun of his slightly slanted eyes and there was no mistaking that he and Dorrine were related. They were the only brown skinned kids with coily East Indian locks of hair, and Oriental looking eyes in the whole school. That, combined with their clothes made him and Dorrine targets. Though the boys knew not to test him unless they wanted to fight, there was a group of girls that used to tease P.J. and say "I wouldn't touch Peter by the hairs of my chinny... chin...chin." Then they would laugh right in his face which made him that much angrier because he couldn't hit girls.

While PJ fought and to a certain extent endured it, there was only so much Duane would be willing to take before he'd end up fighting. Duane was getting sent to the principal's office at least once a week for some sort of disruptive behavior. From the time the twins were able to make a fist, Jean had taught them how to fight. Both twins were able to fight well but where Paul would only fight enough to defend himself or get a kid off him.

Duane on the other hand loved to fight and always threw the first punch in a brawl. While Duane was in the seventh grade, one day a kid named Steven who was a bully picked a fight with him. Steven dwarfed the other kids in the class due to the fact that he had been left back three times. In the seventh grade, he stood at six feet weighing nearly two hundred pounds and was only fourteen. He pretty much physically dominated all of the smaller kids in his class. Steven had heard of Duane while he was still in the sixth grade and how much of a tough guy he was supposed to be. Stephen wanted to claim the crown of being the seventh grade's Billy bad ass in school by beating Duane up.

What people didn't know is that Jean beat Duane for all the times he thought it wasn't imperative for him to fight and this was about eighty five percent of the time. Jean taught his kids only to fight when there wasn't any other option. He also taught them to never back down once they had to fight. Jean taught them to fear only him and what he'd do to any of the boys including P.J. if he found out that any one of them ran coward from a fight that needed to be fought. What Jean didn't know is that Duane developed a high threshold for pain and would only be acting like the beatings he got for fighting were hurting now. Duane didn't want any trouble at home that year so he vowed to do his best to stay out of trouble in the seventh grade.

It was the third week of school in late September of 1984 and Steven tried every trick in the book that he knew to provoke Duane to fight him. Steven was a brown skinned kid with an even Cesar haircut and stood at six feet weighing nearly two hundred pounds and was only fourteen. He was a giant compared to the rest of the kids in his class. Since Duane was trying to stay out of trouble, Steven was doing a number of things trying to provoke a fight with Duane but none of them worked. That is until one day a very cute brown skinned girl named Kiesha Dunne whom Duane had a huge crush on asked him why he had such a funny last name. He explained that he was Haitian on his father's side. Steven overheard their conversation and saw his golden opportunity to finally get Duane to fight him.

The very next day at recess right before the bell rang for class, Steven went around several of his classmates asking. "Do you have H.B.O.?"

Some said yes but Steven stared them down with a scowl on his face and told them that they didn't have it. Then he came over to Duane with a straight face and asked him did he have H.B.O. The trick question trapped Duane as he answered ...

"Yeah, I have H.B.O. My family just got it over the summer and we watch it all the time."

Steven proceeded to make a huge spectacle by announcing. "See y'all I knew it…I just knew it! Not only does this kid have a funny last name like Bapteeeeeste… but he just told you out of his own mouth he has Haitian body odor, H.B.O.! "

Steven was laughing his head off purposely dragging the name Baptiste out to add extra emphasis and insult to ridicule Duane. All the kids in the playground including Kiesha began laughing hysterically at Duane. The bell rang and everyone started running in for their next class, leaving Duane no time to respond to Steven's wise crack.

Once every one came to class the teacher began teaching a lesson on integers. All Duane could think about was all the kids laughing at him and fighting. Steven was gloating, feeling like he got Duane's goat and sleeping because to him it was all one big joke. He never figured on Duane doing anything while school was in session.

Duane knew it was stupid to sit there fuming and decided to go roam the hallways to take his mind off it till he took care of business later. He raised his hand and asked to be excused to the bathroom. His teacher Mrs. Ginsburg waved him up to her desk, without stopping the lecture and gave him the hall pass. He was on his way out the door when he heard Steven who was on his right hand side of the isle blurt out "H.B.O." and make a loud snorting sound from his nose as to mimic a pig. The whole class once again erupted in complete laughter, however Duane wasn't laughing.

Without even thinking Duane grabbed an old abacus Mrs. Ginsburg had along the side counter and began violently bashing Steven about his head and face with it. He hit Steven so hard with it that after several times, the wooden beads that were used to count came off. He broke the abacus on Steven's face. Still enraged, he threw the broken piece across the room and started slugging Steven about the face with his fist. The room filled with crunches and girls screaming as he hit the giant boy in his eyes, nose, throat and temple.

His father had thought him the combination was deadly and only to be used in extreme circumstances but in his blind fury he only saw red, he couldn't think a thought beyond the fight. Everything happened so fast the teacher didn't have the slightest chance of stopping Duane. Then, the horror of the blood flying from Stevens head and globs of blood all over Duane and the walls stopped all reason. She pushed past the horrified students watching and ran down the hall to get two school safety officers.

Nobody dared approach Duane, Steven had dropped out of the chair and curled up on the floor in a semi fetal position yelping, begging for mercy as he covered his head. He was apologizing, dangling on the verge of unconsciousness. Duane was in a trance like state blinded by rage and spewing expletives which no one could understand. People who go to church would have probably said that he was speaking in tongues or may have been possessed by the Holy Ghost.

It took two adult male guards to get the twelve year old, 120 pound, five foot five Duane off the bully who outweighed him by nearly one hundred pounds. They broke the fight up and had to call an E.M.T. unit for the battered bigger boy who had numerous head injuries. The ambulance arrived and immediately rushed them to Miriam Immaculate Hospital. Winsome was almost finished with her shift as she walked through the receiving area of the triage.

There was a buzz as the ambulance indicator in the hospital's bay sounded and everyone available handling stats came forward. E.M.T's rushed two boys into the building from the ambulances they were in. At first it didn't register all the way that it was Duane being pulled out of the ambulance and dragged into the triage. She only saw the bloody and bruised boy being wheeled in on a stretcher. All the kids dressed the same but as she looked closer she remembered the Lacoste polo shirt, and Lee Jeans the boy had on was the same as the outfit she'd saw Duane to go to school in that morning before she kissed him goodbye for school that day. Then great horror set into Winsome's heart when she came to the realization that it actually was her son!

"Animals!" The other nurses were saying.

"Two children fighting in school like that. What kind of people are these? One boy even grab up a weapon!" The primarily West Indian women working there were disgusted and ready to condemn what they thought was Black American savagery when it was really one of their own.

Winsome had been working in the hospital for several years by now, and had gotten used to seeing people come into the hospital alive and leave out dead. So many things ran through her mind at once and she became immediately hysterical once she realized the boy was her own son. She couldn't believe that he too was caught in a cycle of violence that she left Jamaica to escape. She worked two double shifts a week so her boys could have the best things in life. How could this be happening to her boys she thought? A split second later she ran over to where Duane was and yelled out.

"Duane! Duane, what happen to you?" Patients and co-workers were in shock at the scene of the wild looking boy covered in blood and stood watching as Duane tried to calm his mother down.

"Calm down mom…I had a fight in school and everything is o.k. …everything is fine mommy…please stop crying…please." Duane pleaded with his mother as he hopped off the stretcher that the E.M.T. forced him to sit on until he was able to see a doctor.

Winsome regained her composure and asked Duane exactly what happened. He explained that he was in a fight at school and the other kid on the stretcher was the one he was fighting. He also explained that the blood that was all over the place wasn't his but the other kid's blood. Winsome went through a rapid range of emotions from feeling relieved knowing that Duane would be fine to being angry that he was in another fight. However, as a parent she felt pity for the other child and his family. Once it settled in her mind that her son was going to be alright she turned to go into the emergency room where they'd taken Steven to aid the doctor in caring for the child her son had beat to a bloody pulp.

Before she could leave officers from the 131st precinct which was only three blocks away from Duane's school arrived to ask question about the fight. They surveyed the other boy's injuries and started questioning Duane. Once it was confirmed that Duane wasn't injured and indeed had been the one in the fight he was told to come with them. He was to be immediately remanded into the custody of the Queens County Family Court.

Though Winsome was embarrassed beyond measure, angry with her son and still processing what had happened. She felt fortunate the facility they were taking him to was only about two blocks away from the hospital on Parsons Boulevard and not upstate somewhere. Duane was to be held in custody until the next day when he could see a Bureau of Child Welfare (B.C.W.) agent, a counselor, and then finally a judge who would ultimately decide his fate. Winsome left immediately after the police told her they were going to be taking Duane, and contacted her husband at work. Once they both arrived at the family court building they were told they wouldn't be able to see their son until the next day when he was supposed to visit with a counselor. There were so many other children who were already scheduled to see the proper authorities before their fate could be decided that cool and breezy fall afternoon.

Winsome was upset beyond any measure and so was Jean however, he knew he couldn't visibly show it under the circumstances. He was just trying to keep a cool head even though he was truly going insane inside. Jean's existence revolved around his children, his wife, himself, his art and his career and in that exact order. In Jean's eyes, his son becoming a product of the system which he served five days a week was simply not a viable option. He told Winsome not to worry he had a plan that would possibly get Duane off the hook.

There was nothing else for Jean and Winsome to do but go home that evening. However, Jean had grown very close to Judge Blackwell over the years on a professional and personal level. He knew that if he really needed it he could ask his mentor for a huge personal favor. He also knew that the judge would do all in his power to help him in any situation in which he was able to aid him. It just so happened that this was a situation where in which he knew for a fact he'd need the Judge's help.

Jean called Judge Blackwell and explained the gravity of his son's situation. The judge assured him his son would get off with only a slap on the wrist. He had several close associates who worked in the family court system that he'd call on for a favor. He told Jean that as long as he and his wife showed up for the 11:30 A.M. meeting with the family counselor, and B.C.W, (Bureau of Child Welfare) agent that everything would be fine. The next day when they got there they were asked a series of questions by the authorities. Questions such as did their child have any problems at home and what caused him to go off in the manner in which he did?

Duane was present at this time and explained to the court appointed counselor that Duane was a good kid but the constant bullying was why he reacted the way that he did. After they were finished speaking, the counselor explained to Duane's parents that they considered what had happened to be very serious and because of the violence Duane was looking at time in Spotford. He had mercy though because he understood what the young boy was going through and would recommend instead that in order for him not to be taken into the custody of the system he'd have to complete an anger management course as part of his court plan. He'd have to fully complete the course and stay out of trouble with the law for a whole year.

Of course, Jean and Winsome were more than happy to quickly agree to the terms of the court appointed deal. The B.C.W. agent warned them of what could happen the next time Duane got caught. She had seen cases like this before, she said and "these kinds of kids offend and reoffend until they end up in prison for killing somebody". If she had it her way, she would never give second chances.

Jean and Winsome were angry at her characterization of Duane and were about to get into a heated confrontation over the insult. Then Jean thought better of it and decided to save his words for court if he had to speak. He realized the woman had been trying to provoke them to make the case that the whole family was violent so she could recommend he be put in a boys' home. Some caseworkers lived to suck new blood into the system.

In the courtroom, Duane and his parents were nervous at the twelve thirty appearance in front of the judge. They were made for a while until Duane's name was called and everyone was summoned into the judge's private chambers behind closed doors. His name was Judge Gordon and he was an old golfing buddy of Judge Blackwell. He was expecting a visit from the Baptiste clan because his colleague had already asked him to let the boy go with a slap on the wrist. Judge Gordon kept an extremely stern facial expression at all times and Jean feared for a minute something had gone awry.

His facial expression made him very hard to read, and frankly scared the living daylights out of Duane. Duane thought by the look on his face that he was about to be sent away for sure. Judge Gordon began by warning him that if he saw him in his court again, he'd be sent directly to Spotford Youth Detention Center up in the Bronx. The Judge was very frank with Duane and didn't bite his tongue or mince his words one bit.

He told Duane that without question, he'd be easily looking at least a year in Spotford for assault. He explained that Steven's parents had agreed to drop the charges against him as long as they were compensated for their medical expenses and the hours that they'd missed from work for that day. The judge agreed to the anger management court plan. The judge didn't budge while he was grilling Jean and his son all the while slamming his left fist on his desk as to vehemently drive his point home. Jean nodded his head in agreement with the Judge and calmly gathered his family to leave after being dismissed from the Judge's chambers. Once they left the family courthouse and got around the corner into their car, the shouting started as soon as all the doors to the family's second hand Chrysler Plymouth closed.

"Boy, what the fuck is the matter with you? How you go beat a youth in school until he need fi go to the hospital?" Winsome stated in a very rare profanity laden tirade.

"Winnie enough is enough, didn't the boy just spend the night in jail of all places...well didn't he? That's enough for right now, I'll deal with Mr. Duane personally when we get home." Jean said in a firm tone.

"But mi miss a day of work to deal with this foolishness, we are raising him better than that, and work hard..." Winsome started again before being abruptly cut off by Jean.

"Woman I said enough is enough!" Jean yelled at her, stopping Winsome dead in her tracks.

Everyone remained silent in the car for the rest of the six mile ride to their house on 178th Place between 119th and 120th avenue. The only thing in the car making noise after Jean had to raise his voice was the sound of the radio. Jean-Paul very rarely had to raise his voice to his wife especially in front of his children or in public. However, whenever he did, there was absolutely no question about who wore the pants in their family.

As soon as they arrived home, Jean told Duane to go take a shower and get himself together, then come out on the front stoop so they could have a man to man talk. Duane did as he was told and grabbed a snack from the kitchen before he went to meet with his father. When he arrived at the front of the house Jean was waiting for him drinking a Guinness Stout beer. Duane already knew before he came outside that whatever his father was going to tell him would probably be deep.

He also knew that what he was going to say would be more than the usual when he cracked the door and saw his father sipping the beer. Jean would always sit his boys down and talk to them, especially when they fouled up. However when Jean would have to drink before one of their talks it was usually to calm himself down and keep from half murdering them.

Duane was petrified of what his father would do to him but he knew he had to face the music like a man. The only person Duane was truly afraid of was his father. Not just because of the beating he may get, but because of the things his father would say to hurt him. The worst pain Duane had to encounter in his very brief life was his father's words of disapproval that would lash him to his soul like a Cat-O-Nine Tails whip. Truth be told, by this time Duane feared being scolded by his father far more than getting a beating.

However, much to Duane's surprise when he sat down next to his pop, Jean was calmer than he could have ever imagined. In fact, his father took a bottle of beer from the six pack that was resting between his legs and offered Duane a beer of his own. Duane had a sip of beer his father had offered him here and there, but never a whole beer of his own, let alone a stout. Even though Duane really didn't want any of the beer he took it and began to sip its bitter contents ever so slowly. He thought that if that what it took to keep his father from clobbering him then, why not?

"Listen, my lad I'm telling you what I'm telling you for a reason. Even though your brother was born first, it's plain to see you're more dominant than he is. I know he'll fight if he has to, but you affi pick your battles wisely since you all are getting older. I won't always be around to have these talks here with ounoo... seen? I'm telling you this because Paul and P.J. follow behind every little thing you do!"

"Dem nah always copy you exactly...but in their own way still. You're a leader to dem deh youth, so you must be careful where it is that you're leading them. Right now if you keep doing things like this you're gonna lead them straight into prison...or even worse they'll end up dead because they killed somebody trying to impress you. I know what I taught you, but sometimes it's alright if you walk away...listen ah mi now. Choose your fights wisely!"

"Let me make you know something else... if you affi go to jail that's one thing I can't protect you from. If you get locked up tis' you alone that will do the time... no one else. So remember your old man told you that. I'm not going to beat you now but I'm gonna reason with your momma and tell her the only punishment for you is no outside for two weeks including weekends. That way she won't be as mad at the two ah we, seen?" Jean finished the lecture with a hard pat on the shoulder and went inside leaving his son to think.

Duane shook his head up and down in agreement with his father's soliloquy. With a slight smirk on his face and a tingling feeling of pride that stretched from his chin back to the top of his Adams apple. He was proud that his father spoke to him as a man, and not like a little boy. He surely knew that he was far from being his father's equal. However by his father sitting him down and speaking to him to educate him on an aspect of life like a man made him feel warm inside. Plus the fact that his father said that he was a leader gave him ammunition to want to watch himself and do the right things and what was best for his brother, and younger cousin.

Jean went into the house with mixed emotions. He was happy that through Judge Blackwell's intervention he was able to get his son off the hook...this time. At the same time, he knew that if Duane did something a little more serious, he would one day really go to prison. There'd be nothing that they really could do for him. He felt a trifle bit helpless though. He knew that if something was a part of a person's destiny there was nothing that he could do to re-write the history that a person predicted and was writing in advance for themselves.

Jean really hoped the stern talk he gave to his son would do the trick and snap him out of his thug tendencies. He truly wanted his son to heed his warning, because he saw the negative effect the system had on young men and their families every day at work. As a responsible father who was in his children's lives since the day they were born he didn't want his young to be caught up in that vicious cycle. He knew that once you entered the system that there was a good chance that you'd be in and out the system for years to come. He vowed to himself to do everything possible within his power to never let his boys taste the revolving door that people call the criminal justice system.

Jean spoke with his wife at length in regard to their son's situation. He said that he'd rather lose a day at work, and pay whatever fines they had to pay than to see his son caged like a filthy animal behind bars. They settled their differences in terms of Duane's discipline. Jean gave Winsome an endearing kiss on the forehead and wrapped her in his warm embrace to show his love for her and smooth things out for having to raise his voice at her earlier.

Even though, they were well into their second decade together they didn't just love one another they still were deeply in love with one another as if their love was still brand new. Jean felt inspired to be his very best every morning when he'd look into Winsome's gorgeous face. And Winsome fell madly in love with him for the first time all over again with the dawn of each day she spent with him. The beauty of what they shared was rare indeed…a true love of a lifetime.

Duane had been suspended from school for two weeks following the fight with Steven. Normally an outburst like that would have gotten the average student expelled but Duane wasn't the average student. He actually was an honor student who maintained a 3.5 grade point average. The only reason he didn't have straight A's is for never getting higher than a B in gym and that bought his average down. People in the school treated him differently when he returned after his suspension. The staff now treated him like he was trouble or a loose cannon. His parents ended up having to pay more than $1,000.00 for the hospital bills and the E.M.T. service.

In the wake of Steven's horrific beating in front of thirty or so of his classmates, which in middle school standards felt like millions were watching, he transferred to another school a few miles away in Rosedale across the Conduit. Duane, on the other hand, was a living legend by the time he returned to school. The kids in his class spread all types of rumors from Steven being knocked out and bloody to Duane being locked up for putting him in a seizure. There was another rumor floating around that Duane had broken Steven's neck when he made him hit the floor. With Steven being out of the mix, it just added fuel to the fire. The rumors went on and on, but always ended up with Duane coming out on top.

Duane captured so much fame from being suspended and fighting Steven that even Paul and P.J. became popular just by being related to him. The word was definitely out to not try Duane or any of his family or you'd risk ending up just like Steven. The incident became so infamous on campus that kids would fight and the loser of the brawl was said to have got "Stevened." His name became synonymous with getting beat to a pulp. Because of that one episode, throughout the rest of his junior high days, no one ever so much as thought of fighting Duane or any of his family and all the hype had made him that much more devious.

By eighth grade, he'd practiced the whole summer to lose his slight accent and was soon able to flip it on and off so when he wanted to he could talk just like the other kids in his class. His brother and cousins followed his lead and lost their accents as well. During his whole summer vacation, after he finished school and his mandated anger management sessions his free time was spent running with his new crew. He hung out with Sherman who went by "Shiz" in the streets and Terry mostly but whoever else rolled was cool.

They were both from the Bedell Houses and he'd known them since he lived on Fitch across the street from the projects. Sherman was a dark skinned kid that stood about five three and who wore his hair low in a one and a half Caesar with waves. Terry was a brown skinned guy about the same height and was considered to be stocky weighing 160 lbs at age 13. Their days were spent riding bikes and admiring the older guys from the projects who were hustling "gettin' money" and trying to lose their virginity. Even though Kiesha Dunne and Duane were now a couple, she still didn't want to go all the way with him as yet.

CHAPTER SIX

The following summer was the summer of 1985 and there was much change in the air. Duane and Kiesha had been an item for a little over a year ever since Duane had come back to school from suspension. Even though Duane was still a virgin, everyone in his crew including his own brother thought since he and his girl had been together for such a long time that they'd "done it." Every time they'd ask him about it he'd just say that Kiesha was his lady not some skeezer and a gentleman never tells. He'd give them all a funny look then they'd all just laugh it off.

Winsome had been selling plates of West Indian cuisine at her job to some of her co-workers as a side hustle. People liked her cooking so much that they often remarked that she should open her own restaurant. She saw how she would bring home an extra $300.00 tax free every week, and after a year of saving, the dividends began to seriously add up. She began to seriously consider the restaurant business as a viable option of employment. She saw that there weren't too many good West Indian restaurants in her community and began speaking with her husband about her idea.

He agreed that it would be a great idea if they could pull it off and told her he would support her 100% whenever she was ready to get it off the ground. That's all Winsome needed to hear, she had an idea of how to get the funds she needed to open the establishment. She called up Gwen to plead with her to make it a family business.

Gwen would be her partner and that way she wouldn't have to wake up at any God awful hour to clean after the Silverman's anymore.

"Yeah Winnie tis a really good plan but where we gonna get the money fi open the restaurant and keep enough stock in it? It cost a whole heap of money fi run tings right you know. Plus we both have mortgages to pay every month." Gwen stated frankly.

"That's what mi try fi tell you! I spoke to Patrick from Friday gone…he tell mi say there is a white man that wants to buy the land momma owned in the country. Over the years the land has become worth a whole heap of money. The White man is British and is prepared to pay us two hundred fifty thousand British pounds for it. In American money, that's about three hundred thousand dollars. All Patrick say he wants is fifteen percent for watching the land and setting up the deal. That's only about thirty five thousand American dollars."

"That's a lot of money in Jamaica you know…but after all he's done for us he's more like our big brother than a cousin. After we pay him that will still leave us with over two hundred thousand American dollars, but for the deal to go through I'll need the go ahead from you. So what say you…do we take the money and work for ourselves or do we keep working double shifts for other people, and struggling to pay our mortgages and feed our children?" Winsome stated passionately as if she were campaigning for a seat in politics. When Winsome put it like that it was hard for Gwen to say anything other than yes.

Winsome also told Gwen that Patrick gave her the latest news about Donovan Vassel. As it turned out Dexter's fiancé ended up having a boy and she named him after his father. After decades of terrorizing the countryside, Donavan became even more ruthless since the death of his son. Patrick told her tales of his atrocities and his efforts to groom little Dexter into an exact copy of his himself.

Many thought he would've seen what happened because of the way he'd spoiled Dexter but the opposite had happened instead. Donovan's chickens had finally come home to roost. He'd been killed in a bloody ambush…by one of his own henchmen. It turned out that the guy who shoved a shotgun in Donovan's mouth while he was sleeping and woke him just before he blew his head off, worked for Donovan for years just to get close enough to win his family's trust and kill him.

The guy's name was Bashir and he was the young son of one of the men Donovan had murdered at Back o' Wall gully many years earlier for not protecting Dexter. Bashir learned the ins and outs of Donovan's operation to dismantle it and start his own crime family. Being as though he'd murdered the Don Gargon he was automatically royalty in the slums and garrisons of Kingston. All the young hooligans who needed work followed him now. Donovan's younger brother had become head of the Vassel clan and was currently in a very bloody and heated war with Bashir and his goons. It would be combat on the streets of Kingston that rivaled Vietnam any time the rival factions saw one another. They would often exchange gunshots in broad day light killing many innocent bystanders as if neither side had ever heard of police.

After digesting all of what Winsome had to say in regard to the deal that Patrick was brokering she had no choice but to agree. However after hearing what happened to Donovan she still couldn't bring herself to feel any remorse for anybody with the last name Vassel. Gwen and Winsome got back on the phone with their cousin the next day to set up the deal. The next week all the papers they needed to sign came to Winsome's house. They signed the papers and gave Patrick the routing number of her bank and all the other vital details he'd need to wire the sisters their share of the money.

After taxes, Patrick's share and bank fees Gwen and Winsome made out with two hundred fifty thousand American dollars. They agreed to invest half of the money in the business and split the rest for personal reasons. Gwen used the bulk of her money getting ahead on her bills and redecorating her house. She took her kids to the dentist, bought some knick knacks for the house, got some life insurance and put the rest to her kid's college fund. Winsome also decided to get ahead on her bills and splurge on her family. She also put money away in a compound interest account for the twin's education. Paul had also managed to pull his act together and take his c average up to all B's as well on his last report card. She wanted to treat them to some new clothes.

She didn't really want to let go but had to admit to herself that day by day the boys were becoming young men more and more. At thirteen maybe it was time to stop dressing the boys alike. She had to start letting them pick out their own clothes for a change so they could develop their own personalities and be who they were going to be as they came of age. She took them to the Queens Center Mall on Queens Boulevard in Elmhurst and let them pick out what ever clothes they wanted including four pairs of sneakers a piece.

She wanted nothing but the best for her boys, and didn't want them to run the streets and risk going to jail to get the things they wanted. After they were done at the Queens center mall she took them to Green Acres mall in Valley Stream for more shopping and a movie. On the way out the mall Duane saw a pair of frames in the eye glass store that he'd been bugging his mother to buy for a whole year already.

She didn't want to because he didn't need them; however Winsome ultimately relented to her sons' pleas. She purchased the pair of black Cazells he'd been bugging her for but she always said they were too expensive. Once she got a pair for Duane she also had to get a pair for Paul or she'd never hear the end of it. After everything was said and done between taking the boys to the movies, eating at Sizzlers, and buying all the clothes they wanted she ended up spending twenty five hundred dollars on them that day. Indeed it was a lot of money to spend in one day but she felt like nothing was too good for her kids!

The following weekend she sent the twins over to China, and Gwen's while she and Jean took a much needed break and spent the entire weekend down in Atlantic City. They got a hotel suite at the Tropicana. By day they walked the board walk acting like they were teenage lovers lost in the moment. In fact, with them being alone on the beach it reminded them both of the time they spent together on the beach in Port Royal many years earlier.

They were well into their second decade of being together. Yet times like this reminded them both why they fell in love with each other all over again. So many years had passed but every time they made love it was satill as good as the first time. By night they played the slots at the Tropicana, as well as at Bally's and took in several shows before the weekend was out. By and by they had a ball. Times like these made it worthwhile living in America.

A couple of weeks had passed before Winsome and Gwen could find a suitable location for their new joint venture. After three weeks or so they finally decided to use a real estate broker who rented commercial properties. They contacted a real estate firm named Sherwin Reality that they found in the yellow pages. They made an appointment to meet with the agent who happened to be one of the owners of the family run operation. Mr. Sherwin was a thin slick talking Guyanese man of mixed African, and East Indian ancestry. He had olive brown skin a gold front tooth and curly hair with a slight touch of grey on the side of his left side burn.

When they arrived at his office and he discovered that the sisters were fellow West Indians, he felt a sense of pride. He was delighted to see that people of Caribbean roots were making such power moves in the community. In fact he told them of a property on Liberty Avenue and Sutton Boulevard that they could all go see together. When they got to the location the building was in a dilapidated condition and looked to be abandoned for quite some time.

Even though the place was in shambles Winsome could see the potential that the location possessed. They were only about three blocks away from the Long Island Rail Road station, which generated much foot traffic. Plus they were also on a major avenue that was accessible by car. They struck a deal for the twenty five hundred square foot store for four dollars a foot. In the end, after negotiating a three year deal at that rate it cost them thirty thousand dollars just to rent the space. Even though they spent thirty thousand in cash which was approximately a third of what that had to spend, they both agreed it was well worth it because they knew it was going to be a very successful venture.

Winsome who was still working at the hospital changed her hours to nights only for the remainder of the summer. By day, Winsome along with both her sons, nephew and niece would clean the building. By night, after they'd come home for a few hours and had a chance to eat and take a brief nap, Jean and China would both contribute to the labor. With every one's help it took about two and a half weeks to accomplish the desired look. While they were making the final cleanup effort, Winsome ordered all the necessities for the kitchen she needed. Industrial sized pans, ovens, freezers, and stock for the restaurant nothing fancy just the basic things they needed.

Before she knew it Winsome and Gwen ended up spending another twenty thousand just getting the proper materials and licenses from the city. The remaining money in their fifty thousand dollar budget went to get the awning for the front several booths so people could come in and eat and for promotional items and per diem. The day came for them to name the restaurant and raise the awning in front of the store when both sisters realized they hadn't thought of a name for the store. They started telling Dorrine to go and get something out of the car when it struck the both of them what to name it. Since they'd be using their mother's recipes they'd name it after her…that would be the name of the restaurant "Dorrine's."

By this time in 1985, there had been a large influx, and mass migration of immigrants from the Caribbean. Many of them would ride the Subway and Long Island Rail Road, which were both only three to four blocks away a from their location. Winsome and Gwen would have the kids pass out flyers in the vicinity of the train station, on Jamaica Avenue and all throughout south side of Queens in their travels. Winsome, Mrs. Willcott as well as her niece Ronette came to Iceline's to work in the kitchen as cooks. The whole environment was very warm and family oriented.

Winsome put the word out about her new business at her job, and told everyone who bought plates from her that they could come there now to eat and have a wider choice of menu. By far the most popular dish on the menu was the Jerk Chicken, and only after about a month or so they began to do very brisk business. Winsome couldn't believe all the money that the restaurant was making. In just two months, Iceline's had grossed twenty five thousand dollars in sales almost their whole investment for the three year lease. Seeing all that money so quick made Winsome and her family work even harder.

Things were rapidly changing for the twins and their crew as well. By that time crack cocaine was having a major impact in major cities throughout America and hitting hard in every borough of New York City. The drug trade had rapidly turned average guys into neighborhood super stars. South Jamaica was no different.

Kids who weren't even old enough to get licenses were earning enough to purchase the latest Bonnevilles, Caddys and other expensive name brand automobiles with no problem. Often times, young street hustlers would make twice what both their parents would make in a whole year's time in a few weeks standing on a corner or behind a building. The drug money and the lust for it, as well as the breakdown of the family caused by the crack addictions were changing the whole society.

That type of earning power was alluring and it made it very hard for poor kids to turn down the opportunity to make fast cash when they'd never had any before. Especially when they'd learned in this society that money would solve all of their and their family's problems.

Bedell Houses, where Sherman, Terry and their other crimey Junior lived was a major hub for the drug trade in southeastern Queens. There were other parts of Queens and South Jamaica where guys were making a killing but none of the other crews had the organization that Bedell Projects did. The heads of the main group of dealers were only between twenty and twenty four years of age. They called their organization "The Family" because the leaders of their team were brothers and their immediate circle of captains and lieutenants consisted of their cousins.

The bosses of the crew were the third generation of their family to call those projects home. They knew the projects better than they knew themselves. The livest crew was run by Link and Germaine or Germ for short. Link was brown skinned, slightly muscular with a low three sixty wave haircut, he stood about six one and maintained a cool in control demeanor with a serious look on his face at all times. Germ was a couple of shades lighter than Link and was also about six feet tall, he wore his uncommonly long hair in immaculately neat braids, and he always kept a serious look on his face as well.

They were the third consecutive generation of career criminals in their family. Their grandfather was Slick Willy who'd made his money running a bootleg liquor operation and an illegal numbers lottery called Bolita. Their father Lil Willy made his money in reefer, cocaine, and heroin. Now, they were coming of age peddling powdered cocaine, crack, and heroin here and there. Being as though their blood family were well known and respected in their area Link and Germ just followed the example that was already blueprinted for them. The only career their family ever knew was crime and both had been groomed to take over their family's empire since they were small children.

Even though their father Willy had been incarcerated for the past eight years in Wyoming correctional facility on several charges stemming from distribution of an uncontrolled substance, he made sure that he gave his sons his heroin connection in Chinatown. Ted had a direct connection with a Chinese Triad called the Wong's who could get whatever you needed fresh off the boat or plane as long as you were buying large amounts. Through the Wongs, the family was able to put out some of the most potent heroin in the entire borough of Queens. They labeled it "Seventh Heaven" and it could be stepped on ten times before it was bagged and still have the junkies nodding and begging for more.

At twenty four, Link, who was the oldest son, ran the family business. Germ was twenty three and the second of the two children his parents had produced since their high school sweetheart days at John Quincy Adams. Their father had put them on at eighteen and nineteen years old but the Wongs watched them for two years before fully taking them on as partners.

By the time they turned twenty and twenty one respectively they were easily retailing a kilo of product in the street every week. The Chinese had no choice but to take their longtime business associate's offspring seriously and upgrade the amount of product they were willing to give them on consignment. The brothers followed their father's rules, regulations and blueprint on how to make their organization a smashing success. Thus, they were both solidified as legends throughout their borough by the time they were twenty three and twenty four.

In the eighties, "Reaganomics" ruled and on the streets, coke was king. So The Family changed their main interest from boy, or dog food (nick names for heroin) over to girl, or coke as well as its new counterpart crack in late 1984. Drug dealing was a danger filled business all around and without fail, some of the Family's most reliable runners would get caught up by Johnny law and sentenced to three to five year terms. There was always another young Black kid with nothing but lint in his pockets in line to take their place.

People knew better than to snitch and none of The Family's cohorts who got caught ever revealed to law enforcement the source of their product. Not only because that kind of information stayed with Link and Germ but because The Family was well organized and extremely violent! There were so many people getting money with them that anyone who wanted to snitch risked telling the wrong cops and finding themselves face down in a ditch somewhere. Even prison wasn't beyond their reach and the killers on their payroll could touch anyone on the streets as well as prisons all over the city and especially upstate.

Link and Germ decided to start recruiting little kids twelve to sixteen to run certain packages and conduct low level business for two reasons. For one, they'd get by the cops a lot easier, and two they couldn't comprehend the risks they were taking and they were fearless. No matter how brutal they were they still had a child's mentality. Also, most had grown up without fathers, in homes headed by single mothers. They thirsted to be part of something and to have male guidance and direction, even if it was in doing negativity.

For the first time in their lives, they were now able to help put food on the table, buy their little brothers and sisters clothes and shoes and fix up their mother's homes and impress all the girls. When they did get caught they'd only be charged as juveniles and usually get a slap on the wrist with little to no time served. By the summer of 1985, the two brothers had their cousins and other workers keeping an eye out for little kids with heart who'd make good recruits. Sherman was distantly related to Link and Germ. His second cousin Donnell was a first cousin to them and he got put on when school let out that summer. Then it was only a matter of time after Sherman started earning $150.00 a day for running errands and packages for Donnell that Terry and Junior followed in his footsteps.

The first part of the summer of '85, Paul and Duane had been so busy passing out flyers for the restaurant that they didn't have any time to hang out with their boys. They were caught up in eating well and maintaining with the family and the furthest thing on their mind was what was going on in Bedell. By mid-July however, the novelty of the restaurant had passed and they got around to checking for their friends again. Things had changed rapidly in only a month's time. Duane and PJ went up to Sherman's building in the projects and saw him coming out the elevator as soon as they opened the door in the building's lobby.

He looked a lot different than the last time they'd last saw him about three or four weeks earlier. He still looked the same physically it's just that now he was fresh from head to toe. He was wearing a crispy white terry cloth Kangol bucket hat, black Cazell frames a white I-Zod polo top with shorts to match and white and blue Bally's sneakers that appeared to be fresh out the box. Not only was he dressed fresh but there was a group behind him coming out of the elevator and they were fresh as well.

Sherman greeted them ecstatically and as they walked out they building everyone they saw, from kids in their age group to people who were much older received saluted the young men and slapped his palms hard. Sherman had grown up there and was of course well known in his area, but was normally treated like a pest by the older crowd. Now all of a sudden they were treating him like a prince Duane and PJ couldn't help but notice that.

"Yo' what up y'all...long time no see!" Sherman said as he arranged his shirt to sit on the back of one of the courtyard's benches.

"Dag what up Shiz, what you been into lately? What? You the man now?!" Duane wanted to know how Sherman went from shit to sugar so quickly.

"Oh y'all don't know? Man, I'm down with The Family now cold gettin' paid!" Sherman shamelessly boasted.

"What up with you, killer...I see you rockin' Cazellies and Bally's too." Sherman probed admiring how well dressed Duane was as well.

"Well you know... I got this little thing I'm doing around Kiesha's building with some older cats I know from over there." Duane replied, lying through his teeth. He felt pressured to impress Sherman after peeping his new found status.

"Where at, down in Rosenberg?" Sherman inquired.

"Yeah, over there, around circle three." Duane perpetuated his lie while PJ watched him, not getting involved.

"I hear that, but what you really need to do is come back over here with us where you from and get down with the Family...you know I can put you on if you want me to." Sherman offered. They watched some girls pass and turn and wave at Shiz and his crew on the bench.

"I'll think about it..." Duane's mind was more than made up but he didn't want to look thirsty. "By the way who is 'us'? You got some other cats down with you that I don't know about?"

"Nah man...just the crew you know Terry and Junior and some other cats from the buildings down with this here. Man, we all makin' about a G a week. I make what my pops make in two weeks in a good night," he laughed. "I'm getting that grown ass man paper...If you not makin' that type of bread around Kiesha's way you need to stop playin' and come get down with The Family." Sherman had two thick rope chains around his neck, one with a huge crucifix and another with a Lion head piece with rubies for eyes and a nugget diamond in its mouth. He pulled on them as he spoke, watching the way the shine reflected in his friend's eyes. He got an extra two hundred dollars for every new runner but he also wanted his peoples to get down on his team so his little subset could start building their rep.

"Cool. Like I said Shiz…I'll think about it." Duane wouldn't make it seem easy even though he was hype.

There was a chime and Shiz looked down and checked a beeper, which was the biggest hood status symbol at that time. "Bet, I gotta make this run right quick, just come through when you serious. You too, PJ and oh yeah, bring Paul too!" The two slapped palms and Sherman walked out the courtyard onto New York Boulevard to attend to the person who'd paged him.

Duane's mouth literally watered as he thought of all the things he could buy with a thousand dollars a week. More importantly than that, the juice he'd have in the neighborhood when everyone found out that he was down with The Family.

Shiz was his man and he knew he'd have status in the crew as soon as he got on because of that. He had always been the center of attraction in their little posse since the fifth grade. Sherman had never been on his level on the ladder of popularity in school. He always fancied Sherman to be a couple of rungs lower than him on the ladder of the intelligence department as well.

He felt confused now, that Shiz was getting paid, had a chest full of jewelry on and a beeper, which his parents would never get him. And he had done all of this on his own, without Duane's slightest input. That made him a bit aggravated and he started getting a feeling in his stomach that he never thought he'd have especially toward someone he considered to be his friend. He didn't want to admit it to himself at first, but then all once it struck him. As crazy as it sounded it was actually true…he was jealous of Shiz!

He thought that if Sherman was making that type of money then he could easily make twice that much. He figured it was the rule of thumb since he was better than Sherman at everything else.

"Yo'…you doing something in Rosenberg for real? Why you ain't tell me before? You could have been put me down, shoot. " Said P.J. who still didn't even curse.

"Don't worry 'bout that yo. Just shut your mouth and keep your eyes and ears open around my people then you automatically down with whatever I do!

Duane told him. "Let's go down to 72 park. I heard that they was supposed to be throwing a jam down there today."

Duane's mind was still spinning like a Ferris wheel, thinking about what Sherman just told him. He couldn't believe his ears - a G a week at thirteen, Shiz must be buggin', he thought on the one hand. But then again, how'd he get those sharp wears and props from the older heads? He was seriously thinking of how to rise above Sherman's new found status and street fame.

They walked south on New York Boulevard until they came to Rosenberg Village and 72 park. They could hear the music pumping, and bass vibrating from at least four blocks away. Several disk jockeys with neighborhood fame were playing in the park jam that humid summer afternoon. They were spinning the latest jams from Run D.M.C., Whodini and L.L. Cool J. The DJs wowed the crowd, mixing the songs into one another and scratching the records in time with the beat.

The whole atmosphere of the park jams was fly to him and though he loved everything about rap music, the d.j.'ing was the best part to him. The air was alive as people pumped their fists and danced and breakdancers got in the middle of a circle of dancers to show their moves. These were the days that Duane had been longing for all year. The whole park was jammed with people from as young as ten, to adults well into their thirties. He always saw the who's who of the neighborhood at the park jams, and took bits and pieces of all the older guys' style he admired and mimicked them to form his own would be swagger.

Then, out of approximately four to five hundred people in the park that day he spotted Terry and Junior. Junior, Terry's tag along, was a light skinned kid with freckles and red hair that stood about 5 foot six. Both of them were standing by a large dirt mound near the bleachers trying to sweet talk a group of what appeared to be older girls. Much to Duane's surprise, he saw the girls doing what appeared to be writing down their phone numbers and giving them to Terry and Junior. He absolutely couldn't believe his own eyes...his other two flunkies were hooking up with some fly older girls! He just had to approach them and find out what was going on once the girls left. They were showing all of their teeth, cheesing from ear to ear waving good bye as they descended into the crowd.

"Yo'...yo' what up T, what up June?" Duane said as he approached his friends and extended his hand out to slap palms with both of them. "Those girlies y'all was talking to was kinda def! What up with that?" Terry and Junior wore crisp new Adidas short sets. Their sneakers were pristine white and they both had gold chains around their neck and nugget rings on their fingers.

"Aww man D, you know we tryin' to set it off out here...you know Rosenberg got the illest freaks in the hood. We tryin' to be like you my man...a fella gotta get his sometimes right?" Junior laughed.

"Yeah we gotta get ours too man. What you came down here for? To see Kiesha or something?" Terry asked with a hint of sarcasm in his voice. Kiesha Dunne was considered a beauty and all of Duane's little friends had secret crushes on her.

"It's more like or somethin'…I'm down here chillin' with P.J. ….why?" Duane quickly retorted with bass in his voice noting the sarcasm in Terry's tone.

"Oh nah…cause I saw her on the other side of the community center by those other set of big speakers and thought you was comin' to see her is all." Terry stated shrugging his shoulders in a tone that was a little more in his character.

"Aight bet…I'ma go and check on that then! Good lookin', kid! Oh by the way I just saw Shiz comin' out y'all building and he told me y'all got a lil' thing going with them older cats from y'all projects. What up with that?" Duane inquired of both Terry and Junior.

"You know what up with The Family…we down and we cold getting paid! Where you been all summer when you could have been got down, kid!" Terry stood to his full height, the pride reflected on his whole face. He tapped Duane's chest. "You must be doing a lil' something yourself too, all dipped in Cazellies and them crisp new Bally's. You doing something some place too…or did your people buy all that for you?"

Duane laughed, keeping up the front. "Come on now, y'all ain't seen me all summer just like I ain't seen y'all. Of course I'm making moves on the low too. Y'all know I gotta get minze first off the top!" The two boys slapped palms with him, all laughing. "Shiz told me he wants me to get down with y'all, and come back around the way instead of where I'm getting paper right now. I told him I'll think about it…I'll probably end up comin' back around the way. Then I can show y'all how I get down!"

They chilled for a minute and then Duane gave them five and he parted company with them to begin his pursuit of Kiesha on the other side of the park.

"What up baby?" Greeted Duane as he walked up on Kiesha and kissed her on the cheek. He'd found her in the exact spot where Terry said that he saw her last.

"Nothin' sweetheart, just hangin' with Tasha and Kim playin numbers and Uno." Keisha was surprised Duane was at the park jam but she was happy to see him as always.

"Listen I gotta talk to you 'bout something…I know you got a minute for me right?" Duane put his arm around her, enjoying the looks and stares of the other boys around them.

"Yeah no problem, walk with me over by the basketball court so we can talk and have some privacy." Kiesha said, smiling in his arms.

They reached the basketball court where they still could hear the D.J. blending the acapella mix of New Edition's "A Little Bit of Love" with a boomin' break beat. Only now they could hear each other a lot more clearly as well.

"Listen baby, we been together for about a year now and we still ain't do nothin' yet. You keep telling me you ain't ready…and I hear all that, but check this out here I'm down with The Family now and I'm cold getting paid. There's a lot of older fly girls and skeezers that be trying to get with me, but I be telling them I got a girl. Then I have to think to myself why am I with you… and you be cold frontin' on me."

Kiesha was crestfallen but Duane continued. "I'm not tryin' to play you, but these skeezers make it hard to be loyal. I'm not even gon' lie to you, they really be tempting me. I like you a lot but I'm gonna have to let you go, 'cause I don't wanna do you wrong with all these females that keep hawkin' me." Duane said as he kissed her on the cheek as if he were saying good bye and he was actually breaking up with her.

Her face went through a series of emotions. Kiesha looked as though she might cry from the intense pressure and confusion and there was a plea in her eyes when she responded in a crackling voice, "Duane, don't leave me like that! I said I wasn't ready before, you ain't never say nothing about right now. Why is you dissin' me like that? You know I like you a lot!" Kiesha's young mind was blown away by what Duane had just stated. Feeling pressure to keep her boyfriend and not lose him to some other girl she impulsively made the split second decision to give Duane her Cherry.

"Yeah I like you a lot too just make sure you doin' it cause you want to…not no pressure." Duane slyly stated, knowing he had her right where he wanted her.

"I'm not, Baby." Kiesha lied. "I really mean it. I been wantin' to bring it up since school let out, but I ain't been seein' you and I didn't know how to tell you over the phone." Kiesha tried to sound sincere but she was really fearful. She felt so confused.

"Word I hear that… just make sure that you don't fess on me when it's time to get busy." The smooth young charlatan matter-of-factly stated.

"My moms is at her new job in Garden City way out in Long Island, and my sister is caught up with her man at the jam. Ain't nobody gonna be at my house at least until the jam is over, and that ain't for at least another three or four hours. Do you want to come over right now?" Kiesha said telling Duane just exactly what he wanted to hear.

They dropped P.J. off at a bus stop then began walking to building nine in section three of Rosenberg Village which was on the other side of the complex from the park jam. It only took about ten minutes to walk to where Kiesha's building was, but to Duane's raging hormones it felt more like an eternity.

They got to her building and walked through the lobby and to the elevator which they took to the eighth floor to Keisha's family apartment of 8d. Once they were in the two bedroom apartment they made their way straight to her bedroom which she shared with her older sister Tennille. They sat on her bed and began kissing and heavy petting. They both were very nervous and excited. Kiesha's heart was dancing on the back of her tongue when after ten minutes she finally got up the courage to break away from Duane's embrace to begin taking off her clothes. She took off her red jelly sandals first then her blue jeans and white blouse briefly revealing her bare ebony frame before she quickly scurried under her comforter they were both sitting on.

After Kiesha was under the comforter she took off her unmentionables and threw them to the floor inviting Duane in with a come hither motion of her right index finger. In just half of a heart beat Duane's clothes were off and he was in the bed with Kiesha. His little soldier was at full attention and he was more than ready to get some mud for his turtle. Duane got under the comforter with Kiesha and couldn't help but notice how soft her skin was as he fumbled and struggled for a moment. About five minutes later they finally began going through the motions and Duane tried to play it off as if he were a pro but was still stumbling and bumbling to no end.

Even though both of them got a kick from the fact that they actually were "doing it." Duane enjoyed the fact that he was able to manipulate Kiesha's young mind just as much and if not more. Twenty minutes after they started grunting and moaning they began getting dressed. They'd both left their innocence at the threshold of Kiesha's bedroom door before they went in. At only the tender age of thirteen Duane had begun his journey through manhood and now there was absolutely no turning back.

After they both were dressed Kiesha walked him from her apartment to the elevator. After her first time Kiesha was now all in, Duane made her world go around in circles. After waiting a few minutes the elevator came and Kiesha whispered "I love you" before the doors slammed shut. Duane just smirked and nodded his head in agreement with her statement…he was deeply in love with himself as well.

Duane got home and immediately took a hot shower. He was astonished how people treated him. Even Kiesha treated him different when he said that he was down with The Family. He got in his bed and the excitement of the conversation he'd have with Sherman the next day brought a smile to his face. He lay there plotting and scheming at how much clout, currency and girls he would be getting just by merely being down with them.

The following day after he'd finished doing chores around his family's restaurant he immediately found his way to the Bedell projects where he ran across Terry and Junior.

"Yo what up y'all...where Shiz at? Y'all seen him today? I need to talk to him about something."

"He be right back he went to make a run right quick, what you need to talk to him about?" Terry quizzed as he bent over adjusting the cuff on his new Lee Jeans.

"Don't you worry yourself about that son... it's a conversation between grown folks only." Duane flippantly retorted.

"Oh I'm only asking 'cause I told Shiz we saw you at the park yesterday. How you said you was seriously thinking about getting down with the program…Shiz was like bet! He been expecting to see you cause he said them dudes in Rosenberg wasn't treating you right and you need to bring your Bob Marley rass back to where you belong cause he don't trust them dudes in the co-ops." Terry stated playfully knowing only members of his crew could get away with joking about his heritage and not receive an immediate speed knot.

"Oh word! Sike. I'm just playin with you T! Of course I wanna come back around the block. I don't really trust those cats down there in that high priced project no way.

I'm gonna give Shiz a play and come through like I said I was gon think about." Stated Duane boastfully, once again skillfully manipulating his friends to get what he wanted.

"Aight bet, just wait over there on the benches he should be right back, you can speak to him when he come through. We gotta break out to make this run." Terry told Duane as he gave him a pound then began walking toward New York Boulevard with Junior in tow, so they could make a delivery.

He only had to wait about fifteen minutes before Sherman made his grand entrance into the court yard of the projects ditty bopping toward Duane on the green wooden benches. He greeted everyone he came into contact with along the way as if he was the mayor.

"What up D? I see you not playin' around about makin this paper huh…you came through to get down with the program or what?" Sherman asked already knowing the answer to his question before Duane even opened his mouth to reply.

"Nah I ain't come through my area to get down with you…I came to show you how I do!" Duane boldly stated putting Sherman in check, bluffing as if he was already getting money some other place.

"O.K. man…no need for you to try and bass me, you know what I meant by that right D?" Sherman said feeling somewhat chumped because of Duane's seemingly nonchalant response to a proposal anybody else would have jumped at. Plus, he didn't want to see his two hundred dollar bonus to get up from the benches and walk back down to Rosenberg Village to hustle. He'd do Shiz absolutely no good money wise down there.

"Cool …cool then! Check this out, wait right here and I'll run and get my peoples." Sherman said with a smirk on his face as he made his way from where they were sitting and descended into one of the buildings near the basketball courts. About five minutes later he came back out of the building with his older cousin Donnell. Donnell was only five years older than they were but at eighteen he was practically a street veteran to them.

Donnell had a medium build, he was brown skinned and stood about five foot eleven and sported a low Caesar haircut with a part in the middle of his hair. He also constantly sported gold too. This occasion was no different he had on two rope chains, and a Swiss link with a B.M.W. charm. He also wore diamond pinky rings, gold dipped Cazell frames and a Fila track suit with sneakers to match.

Duane was in awe as Donnell approached him, because at that time to wear truck jewelry, let alone in the projects was not only a status symbol but also a respect thing. Not only did you have to have enough money to buy it, you also had to be strong enough to keep it! He knew Donnell, called D in Bedell was down with The Family and he'd heard the rumors of him being tied to a series of murders and being affiliated with the crew's twenty known killers on their payroll. The whole area knew that they weren't to be trifled with, so the stick up kids rarely tried one of their members if at all.

"What up Shorty?" Exclaimed Donnell as he came out of the building with his chains swinging.

"My little cuz say you his man and you ready to step to the A.M.!"

"Yeah…I'm ready to put it down!" Duane shot back swift and emphatically.

"He say you was down in Rosenberg…you probably was fuckin' with Alex and them, hunh?" Donnell stated not trying to hide his disgust for the competition hustling in the Co-ops.

"Well you know I was doin' my thing here and there, but now it's time for me to come back on this side because this is where I was raised." Duane said evenly, as though he wouldn't tell any tales.

"Yeah, punk mothafucka…I ain't never liked his pretty boy light bright almost white lookin ass even when we went to Springfield together! What they had you doing? Probably look out with his cheap ass huh?" Donnell let his disdain for Alex and his crew be shown and well known. Duane didn't even really know who Donnell was talking about so he just nodded his head and went right along with everything he was saying.

"Yeah, I know that cheap mothafucka only be paying his boys $50.00 a day for that, and that's why his faggot ass keep getting knocked! How you gon pay ya people $50.00 a day and expect them to do a good job for you? Man they can make that type of chump change at Mickey D's…sucka ass nigga! Well check this out, my little man I had watching the stash just got knocked the other day and we need somebody just like you. It pays $100.00 a day…you down?" Donnell asked.

"No doubt!" Duane shot back with his chest out, not missing a single beat.

"Cool cause it's real simple! See that building right behind you? That's 118-10 New York Boulevard. Over here we never say street names just the numbers. All you gotta do is make sure there no base heads or housing police coming through the door over there or fuckin' with that trash can right there but me and my peoples…its real fuckin' simple! Matter fact too simple…if anybody outside of me and my people come through that door while we doing business or fuck with that trash can then all you gotta do is yell 118-10 three times real loud so we can hear you. If it's the police, housing or otherwise, just yell soo-wee like you calling a pig…got it?" Donnell explained.

"Yeah not a problem, when you want me to start?" Duane eagerly asked in response.

"Shiiit. Lil' nigga you started when I came out the building!" He cracked a smile and Duane couldn't help but smile too. That was the start of Duane's career as a criminal. Donnell hugged Duane to him and clapped him on the shoulder, hard like a man and told him "Welcome to the family."

Everything went as smooth as Swiss clock work that day. Duane spotted two squad cars from the 131st precinct and housing police cruising through the court yard of the project as if they were going to make a move on 118-10. He whistled "soo-wee" at the top of his lungs before the police could enter the building and everybody jetted in a million directions. They did away with any contraband before the cops could even make their way into the building. Someone had probably called the police about the loitering and them making too much noise in the stairwell of the building or maybe they were just trying to fill a quota. Regardless, no one was trying to get caught and that first close encounter made Duane feel like it was all a game he was playing with them.

The day ended for Duane at about 8:30 after the sun started to go down, then D paid him as promised one hundred dollars in denominations of ones, fives, and tens. Duane couldn't believe it he was actually down with The Family now. It was on the level of a peon, but all that really mattered to him is that he was down. He was successful at faking it till he made it. All he really ever wanted was to be accepted and belong to something he felt like was greater than himself that people admired.

Indeed the dope fiends and base heads may have been hooked to their vice of choice, but Duane had been turned completely out and addicted that day as well. He wasn't addicted to drugs like they were, but to the prestige and fame that being affiliated with The Family brought. He was also infatuated and addicted to street culture as a whole. Even though now he didn't live near the projects or Southside anymore, because of his fascination with the big time hustlers and fly girls and their world, Duane was just as hooked as any of the customers were.

That night when he got home, after he took a shower, he came into his bed room gloating, rehashing all the seemingly incredible events that had taken place in those last twenty four hours. He'd lost his virginity, got down with The Family, and earned his first one hundred dollars in the street as his own man. They didn't know it yet, but by putting Duane on to hustling they had just created a megalomaniac. Duane lay there in his bed staring at the ceiling, plotting on how he was going to achieve taking over the world…or at least South Jamaica and the surrounding vicinity.

Paul was in his room playing with his Caleco Vision when he got the urge and inclination to check on his twin. He could detect that change was in the air. After all they were twins, and had a sort of slight telepathy in regard to one another. They could slightly feel each other's emotions if either one of them got excited enough. He got up and knocked on Duane's bedroom door before he was invited in.

"What's the matter with you why you layin' in bed with just the lamp on, why you just layin in here like that for? I know I didn't just catch you in here beatin' your dick!" Paul said, jabbing at Duane to agitate him. Looking at his brother he knew something was really behind the feeling that he got to make him want to check up on Duane.

"Beat my dick...you sound mega stupid right now! What would I be doin' beatin' my dick when I got a girl? Unlike some people I know!" Duane stated jabbing right back at his brother still holding his trump card about him and Kiesha tight his the chest.

"So what you got a girl that don't mean nothing, you still ain't did it yet. So you might as well not be claiming her as your girl." Paul shot back striving to ground Duane since he was talking fly to him.

"See that's your problem junior, you play too much and talk shit about stuff you don't know anything about...anyway what you want?" Duane said mockingly as if he were older than Peter and in the same tone as if he was putting a member of his little crew in check.

"Nothing really I was just checking on you, trying to see if you wanted to play Donkey Kong or if you scared." Paul knew how to get his brother to do just about anything by playing on his ego.

Duane said nothing, stretched out like a big cat with his hands folded behind his head. Paul had a revelation. "Ooooow....that's why I'm getting this feeling ....you....you...you finally got you some! You got some didn't you? Awww man! Why you ain't say something. When did it happen?"

"Wow! Why don't you say it a little louder... that way if mommy didn't hear you, then the people next door definitely can." Duane shot back with a slight smirk. He was going to make Paul beg for details.

"See all them times we be askin' you if you did it with her, I been knew you ain't do nothing. See me and you got that thing about each other...but I know y'all ain't do nothing yet, I just went along with the program. I been knew you was perpetrating a fraud!" Paul stated in a know it all type of fashion.

"Whatever, I hear you talking all that mumbo jumbo about our connection and all, but I'm a gentleman and a gentleman never tells and a real man wouldn't have to ask what I did or didn't do with my lady." Duane said striving to sound older and more experienced now that he'd navigated his ship of virginity into the unexplored waters of manhood.

"Nigga you sound like a broke ass Billy D. Williams with that trash you spittin'. See I'm your brother, and I know you and I know when something is going on. I don't know what it is…but I'ma find out watch!" Paul stated as both the boys went into his room and played a few games of Donkey Kong before they turned in for the evening.

CHAPTER SEVEN

Approximately a month passed since Duane had been working for big D. Work, as he called it, was never boring but more and more he was learning about the inner workings of the trade and the little dramas he hadn't known about looking at it from the outside in. He hadn't known, for example that The Family was at odds with two separate crews who also sold drugs in Bedell houses. The other crews also controlled three of the eight buildings there in the projects.

The Family had complete control over five of the buildings that were on their side of New York Boulevard one way or another. Whether it was through them directly or through them supplying what brand of drugs people sold on their side of the projects. There had been a few incidents where they'd exchanged a volley of automatic gunfire with a few members of the rival crews from the other side of the projects and its surrounding vicinity. It was bad because it brought the police around but good because the fear they were provoking in people's hearts made them not want to go up against The Family for any reason after that.

Even though they were of the streets and wanted control of the other three buildings in their complex, The Family's business was making money smoothly not warring back and forth for crumbs. They would avoid a long drawn out beef that would jeopardize the security of their main moneymaking operation at all cost. Link put word out through his captains that he had a solution to all the bumping of heads that was making their whole section of Jamaica hot. He told them to call a meeting with the heads of the other crews who operated on the other side of the projects and stress that the key to all their success would be them getting organized under one umbrella.

He mapped out a plan where the captains and lieutenants of the other crews would all walk away feeling like it was a win-win for all. The Family didn't have enough truly dedicated soldiers to man all eight buildings. However they did have enough fire power and killers to make it hard for the other three buildings in their projects to operate. The agreement he was proposing was for The Family to supply them with whatever it was they were selling.

In exchange the Family would call off all their goons and let them operate however they wanted on their side of New York Boulevard while protecting their new consolidated interest if any hostile elements from outside the complex tried to invade any of the three non Family buildings. Link also proposed the same agreement to the crews manning 118-14 New York Boulevard.

Just like they did for the building Donnell ran, Link and Germ would supply all three buildings on the opposite side of the boulevard with a group of workers to work shifts in their buildings if for whatever reason they didn't have enough money for re-up or a police raid. The workers would be there until they earned the amount it would have cost to buy the product that the other crews needed with a twenty percent tax added onto their next package. This way everybody made money, there never would be a drought and the customers would be none the wiser.

Everyone could see the wisdom of this and overnight it went from being killings left and right to a carefully controlled and intense atmosphere of cooperation. This pissed off the powers of law enforcement to no end. Now that Link had successfully annexed their operation into several sub divisions under different bosses it was virtually impossible to shut down the open air drug trade in their projects. The police were only busting low level people who really didn't know who was running the show throughout their area any way. Only the captains and lieutenants like Donnell would deal directly with Link or Germ.

These captains or lieutenants would distribute product and discuss business with the bosses of the newly allied crews and workers in the buildings they controlled. If by chance any of the upper echelon from the other crews they dealt with got busted, no matter how much the authorities would try, they would never give their supplier up. Mainly because they'd be labeled a snitch and have killers to deal with, which wasn't an option they even wanted to think about facing or putting their families in danger of. The drug game had become so murderous that people were not only hurting the person who had violated but killing babies, grandmothers and shooting up whole families. A snitch couldn't make a deal for his extended family, and after he ran, it was known that's who the consequences would fall on.

All in all, The Family now had their hands in the drug trade in the whole project and its surrounding area one way or another. During that summer, it was rumored that The Family netted approximately a half a million dollars every week. So the little thousand dollars they funneled to their low level grunts like Duane, Sherman, and the rest of their crew was inconsequential. However, you couldn't tell them that, they thought they were making big money. By the same token, a grand a week to a young teenager who never had a job and lived in abject poverty was equivalent to them amassing a fortune in their impressionable minds.

Duane was doing his thing, as they say, that summer. He still worked with his family at the restaurant to keep his mother off his back and he was making good money with his job as a look out for Big D. Duane absolutely loved and adored the spotlight he received in the neighborhood from hanging with his crew and making money. Even though Duane didn't make the same amount of money that his boys did for delivering packages it was quite alright with him. All he really wanted was recognition and popularity amongst his peers.

He had already made a name for himself in school and now he was making a name for himself in the street as Little D from Bedell projects. At least that's who he was to people who knew him from his affiliation and alliance with his crew who actually did reside in the projects. That summer came and went, only now when school started in the fall, Duane and his crew was the talk of the town on campus. All the girls who were dating at the time wanted to get with them. Sherman thought he was making so much money at that point that he only occasionally showed up to school and that was only to show off some of his new wears.

Duane had mad love and respect for Sherman but still regarded him as a few notches lower than him. He appreciated Shiz for putting him on even though he wasn't making the same money as the others were, he was down with their program and that was enough. Duane and Kiesha were still going together and whenever her mother wasn't home she'd invite Duane over to play house for a while after school. You couldn't tell Duane anything. His head had swollen beyond measure and he was sure that he was the man.

Even though Terry and Junior were still down with the crew somehow they still never got the same shine as Duane or Sherman. In fact, Duane and Sherman were like two peas in a pod. They became very close after that summer and Terry couldn't stand it one bit, he felt pushed to the side and he resented Duane who to him was several rungs below them as a lookout who wasn't even doing hand to hands like he was.

Terry had known Shiz his entire life and lived in the same building as he did...hell Duane wasn't even really from the projects. This resentment colored their friendship. They were cool but Terry couldn't help making snide remarks towards Duane at times. When he would retaliate and put Terry back in his place, Duane drew laughs from whoever heard and seemingly more popularity, another dagger. The irony of Terry's envy is that he was officially down with the crew yet he acted as if he was an outsider trying to get noticed.

Had he just played his role instead of always talking trash competing with Duane for his position as Sherman's right hand man they would have viewed him as their equal. Junior for the most part stayed out of it and never gave any hint that he detected any undercurrent of petty jealousy. Junior was cool just making money so he could buy himself clothes and feed his younger siblings. His mother was a crack fiend who routinely smoked away her paycheck and sold all of her food stamps to by crack. They were raising themselves and the whole family depended on Junior, who was now not only the big brother but the man of the house. Because of his personal drama, all Junior wanted was to play his position and keep making his daily bread.

Back on the home front, things weren't all peachy keen in China and Gwen's household. With Gwen putting in so many hours at the restaurant and taking care of the kids once she came home, their relationship began to falter. China was several years younger than Gwen and still had a very ravenous libido. In years past Gwen had suspected China of cheating on her, but had no solid evidence to back up her suspicions. However, lately China had begun coming home later and later at all times of the night smelling like a strange mixture of liquor, and different perfumes. She'd also found several different women's phone numbers in China's garments when she washed them.

Gwen had to wake up and smell the coffee, there was no denying it any longer she had to face the fact that her husband had been with other women. China had never really fully given up the tomcatting ways of his youth. Gwen tried to live with it for a while, but finally enough was enough. The straw that broke the camel's back was when some strange woman called the house while the family was all sitting at the dinner table and Gwen answered the phone. Instead of playing it off as though it were a wrong number like the other woman usually did, this one was bold and she tried to give Gwen an earful. After Gwen decimated her verbally, she made up her mind that things with Chinaman were over. It was one thing to know her husband was cheating on her, however for it to be right in her face and to be disrespected in her own home in front of her children was the ultimate deal breaker.

They both faced the music and agreed to separate Gwen was tired of playing a charade for the sake of the children. She just couldn't put on the masquerade any longer after years of suspecting that China was unfaithful. Besides the children were eleven, and twelve years old now they were old enough to understand what was going on. Gwen wasn't doing them any favors keeping him there in a constant state of anger and chaos. So China neatly packed his things and moved in with one of his many mistresses named Susan.

Susan was a dark skinned twenty five year old bombshell of Trinidadian descent that lived in the Flatbush section of Brooklyn. China stayed with her several months until he got tired of her. He ended up getting himself a new job as a super in another building in Flatbush located on east Twenty First Street. He still had his job as a hack driver, and lived rent free since he became a super in the building everyone in the community referred to as The Castle.

The school year flew by and now it was the summer of 1986. In appreciation of all the hard work that Sherman and the boys had put in, Donnell brought them Honda scooters for their eighth grade graduation. Two Sprees for Terry and Junior, and Two Elites for Shiz and Little D. They were superstars in the neighborhood after that. That was it now…there was no turning back for any of them. They were all just fourteen years old and sitting on top of the world. During the time they weren't running packages and playing lookout for Donnell, Duane and company would hang out on Jamaica Avenue or ride out to the beach in Far Rockaway to profile.

The boys in Duane's crew thought Donnell got them the scooters out of the kindness of his heart, but in fact he'd been ordered by his bosses to do so. Even though, no one rarely saw Link nor Germ handling any product they still were aware of every minute detail of their operation. They knew from experience for their operation to be a long term success that they had to keep all their men happy starting from the ground up. They ordered Donnell to get the scooters for the younger loyal guys for two reasons. One was to keep the moral of the youngsters up and give them something to look forward to. In addition it would allow them more maneuverability to rapidly deliver their goods to several different drug strips throughout south eastern Queens.

Due to the absence of China's presence in the house Duane had become more than just an older cousin to P.J. he was more like an older brother and role model. Duane never forgot the lecture his father gave him a few years prior to China moving to Brooklyn and began paying very close attention to P.J. In fact P.J. and Duane started to grow even closer than his own twin brother. Whenever Duane had some free time he always would make sure to meet P.J. someplace and pick him up on the scooter since his parents didn't know he had it, they'd always have to meet in different locations.

All the money Duane was making was spent mostly on taking P.J. and Kiesha different places and buying them different articles of clothing here and there. The restaurant was doing well and Winsome brought so many clothes on the regular that she really couldn't keep up with the little things Duane brought for himself.

As time progressed Duane saw that Terry was growing increasingly jealous of him, even though he earned more money making deliveries, and had his own scooter. Duane had the foresight to see that still wasn't enough for Terry. He began to think he may have to severely hurt him to make an example of him before the summer was over. So he devised a plan that would benefit them both that would probably keep the peace.

When Duane would go home at night he would let Terry hold his scooter, because his parents wouldn't let him have one. Being in the drug game had made Duane unbelievably cunning and there wasn't anything he did that didn't have an ulterior motive. He started behaving and thinking like a leader instead of just talking and acting like one. He could have easily let Junior hold the scooter, but he knew Terry may have done something devious to his ride and then he'd have to seriously fuck him up!

At the end of the summer, Link, Germ and the other older guys they ran with organized basketball tournaments. They supplied uniforms and fed the players and made an occasion of it by having the games coincide with jams in the park. It was in part genuine, they knew the kids liked playing ball and it was a good way to show off Bedell's most talented players but overall, it was more a very measured and calculated business move. This way they didn't look totally like the opportunistic robber barons of the ghetto that they were actually turning out to be. They knew if they gave the kids something to do and threw a few barbecues it would go a long way with the people who resided in their community.

The league was comprised of several teams from the projects in the South Jamaica area as well as teams from Hollis, Ajax Park, Lincoln Park, and Rosenberg Village. The Bedell Houses team consisted of the best players their project had to offer as well as several ringers who didn't live there. Paul, Duane's brother had quite the rep as a baller and to the crew he was a natural for team captain. During his last couple of years in junior high, Paul had become very active in sports and he was "nasty" in basketball. He was getting recruited from the eighth grade and several high schools wanted him to play for their program during his freshman year.

However, due to him lacking the proper grade point average he ended up going to his zoned neighborhood school which was Andrew Jackson. Paul envisioned and dreamed of himself playing for basketball power house Christ the King. He knew since he was from New York that he probably would get the attention he wanted from the division one colleges in the big east conference if he excelled on the court. Then from there, possibly the N.B.A. one never knows he thought.

Donnell had heard a little buzz about Paul but Sherman and Junior drove home the point of how nice he was. Donnell wanted him for the team he was organizing before any of the opposing teams could recruit him as one of their own. Donnell instructed Duane to bring Paul through the courts in the back of his building so he could see his moves in person.

Donnell was acting as a talent coordinator if he liked what he saw in Paul he'd automatically be on the squad. He'd be given a black and gold Jersey that read Bedell in front and had his name on the back. The next day Duane brought Paul to the courts to meet Donnell so he could see how well he meshed with the rest of the local talent The Family was recruiting. Paul hit the court and was a force to be reckoned with. He handled himself immensely well against kids in his peer group as well as several older guys who would be starting college on full scholarships in the fall.

"Alright my man, that's enough I've seen all I need to see."

Donnell said in a flat tone and a stoned face holding a clip board as if he were Pat Riley.

"But I'm sayin' though...you thought I was wack? Give me the ball again I can do better...for real!" Paul stated emphatic and desperately.

"Nah Shorty chill, you buggin out...you was out there bussin' ass! You down with the squad if you want the slot...so what up? You gon play for us or not?" Donnell stated.

Without hesitation, Paul accepted Donnell's invitation. He was overwhelmed with elation because, he knew being on the team was a crowning achievement and he'd be a star in the 'hood. Once they'd all started hustling, he'd gone in the total opposite direction, into sports. Now he would be rolling with The Family too, just in another capacity.

It didn't matter how he was down with The Family, he was down and that's all that mattered. Since he always wore new clothes and Duane was affiliated with The Family people in school assumed Paul must be with them as well. However, now that he was a part of the team the basketball court would be the stage he'd prove himself on in front of The Family, his peers, Duane, and the whole south side of Queens.

"Yo, little D! Why you ain't never tell me your brother was nice with the rock? You should have been told me when you found out we was putting a team together. What's wrong with you Shorty? You gotta get on point and get it together man!"

Donnell stated playfully reprimanding his young protégé.

Duane just stood there shrugging his shoulders with an impish look on his face at a loss for words for once, not knowing exactly what to say. Deep down, he fancied his brother as a square. He didn't want him around the projects because he thought he'd have to constantly protect Paul instead of doing his job as a lookout.

"Yo Shorty, go over there and talk to my man Milton over there by the jeep and he'll take the size you need for the uniform. My man Milt will hook you right on up." Donnell said to Paul after joking with him about his brother.

"Damn I'm sayin' though…since y'all are identical twins how will I be able to tell the two of you apart when y'all are together?" Donnell asked.

"Cause I'm gon be the one about gettin this money while he play Michael Jordan of south side!" Duane playfully said trying to redeem himself for not bringing his brother around sooner.

"Yeah I hear that Shorty...just do your job, and everything will be fine." Donnell said in response.

"Well I guess since he gon have the ball shaking and baking cats, not riding the bench, that's how I'll be able to tell y'all apart. See because you still gon have to be playin' the benches and the court yard doing your job. That's it...that's what we'll call him! Hey yo' Shorty what's your name again? Matter of fact, Little D tell your brother to come back over here for a minute." Donnell said wielding his authority over his minion.

"Yo' come here man, you heard D didn't you?" Duane said showing off in front of his crew, and asserting his position over Paul.

Paul jogged in their direction and came back to where his brother and all the others were standing next to Donnell. "What's up?" Paul quizzed. He was hyped about making the team and wasn't picking up on all the emotional wrangling.

"What's your name again, little man?" asked Donnell.

"Paul." He replied sticking his chest out with a big smile on his face. He felt as high as the first man to walk on the moon because an older guy with status wanted to know who he was.

"I hear that, but it sounds kind of square. It doesn't have a ring to it. See we about to make you into a legend on the basketball court, you gotta have a fly name...at least on the court anyway. So check this out here from now on because of the way you handled the rock we'll call you Shake and Bake...alright Shorty?" Donnell put his arm around Paul, who was positively beaming, savoring the moment.

"Bet that!" Paul swiftly responded.

"Now run back over there by Milt so he can get your size for your uniform and tell him
I said to put Shake and Bake on the back." Donnell wrote Paul's name on the clip board and it clashed against one of his rope chains. Paul happily jogged back to tell Milton his size and brand new moniker.

"Our first game is the Thursday after next we should have the other two spots for the team filled by the end of the day. Our first practice is the day after tomorrow at 7:00 in the evening. You'll be meeting the coach then so make sure you be here on time or be cut from the team. This is serious business...understand?" Milt instructed. Milt was a neighborhood legend. He could have went to the pros if he'd gone to school but since he hadn't, he now had to be content running the park tournaments instead.

A couple of hours later the try outs were done and the whole roster for the team had been selected and now it was back to business as usual for Duane and his crew. The kids were very proud that Paul made the team. They were even more proud because Donnell liked him enough to give him a nick name from the first day he met him. They played Junior's boombox to its capacity grooving to a song on Kiss F.M. called "Games People Play" as they sat on their scooters telling jokes and catcalling after the young females passing by.

Terry also sat on his scooter with a look of indifference on his face. He laughed and chuckled with everyone else and to the naked eye it appeared everything was cool. They had a good time standing there chilling and it wasn't until later Duane detected something was amiss. As he and Paul got ready to leave, he asked Terry to hold his scooter until the next day like they'd been doing since he got it. He played it off like it was no big deal then said his goodbyes to his boys as he and Paul made their way down to Bedell Boulevard and caught the bus home.

When they got home they told their parents the good news about Paul being selected for the team and of course Jean and Winsome were both ecstatic. They hugged him, and told him how proud they were of him and to keep up the good work. They were happy that Paul found a productive outlet for his youthful energy that would more than likely keep him out of trouble. However Winsome was still concerned about Duane getting in trouble that summer if they didn't find anything for him to do as well.

"We need some extra help around the restaurant so why don't you come in a little earlier for a few more hours a day to help out, Duane?" Winsome asked. Duane knew better. He knew if his mother was requesting his service it was more of a demand.

"Nah Ma, I can't. I have to take P.J. to go watch Paul play ball. I want to support him; you know he's gonna be a star one day." Duane said boastfully of his brother's skills also stroking Paul's ego at the same time. He knew he was causing Winsome's head and heart to fill with pride for her boys with the lie that he'd just skillfully spun. Duane knew all the while that he didn't want to be in the restaurant under his mother and aunt all day, he'd much rather be on the block causing havoc.

They all got settled for a late supper of leftovers from the restaurant. The boys washed up, played video games for a while then went to bed still hyped about everything that had happened that day and talking about the big day ahead of them the next day. Early the next morning, Paul started what was to become a daily ritual for the whole summer. He'd get up at seven to do his stretches and pushups, and then have a light fruit breakfast.

At about eight thirty, after he'd finished digesting his breakfast and washing up, he'd jog dribbling his basketball down 120th avenue about six blocks to 120th park on Bedell Boulevard. Once he got there, he'd run suicides for about fifteen minutes then take jump shots from all different angles of the court for two hours. He'd even get up and execute his routine on the days he had practice. It was very rare that you didn't see him with a basketball in his hands after he made the team, because he lived and breathed to play the game now.

Some kids liked the game of basketball and they were good at it, but his desire was different from theirs. They only liked the game while he loved it. He dedicated himself to basketball the same way Duane dedicated himself to hustling and doing whatever it took for recognition in his neighborhood.

He made it to his first team practice at seven P.M. on the dot just as he'd agreed to do. Donnell introduced him to his new coach, God Sincere Allah. He called himself a member of the Nation of God and Earth but the young kids in the area knew them better as the Five Percenters. At thirty two, Sincere was several years older than the eldest leaders in The Family. He also was loved and respected to the utmost by the vast majority of the community at large. He was a brown skinned brother with a one and a half fade hair cut, sleepy eyes and a relaxed yet serious demeanor. He stood about five foot ten and was built like a tank wearing gold frame glasses, a small rope chain, and a sky blue nylon B.V.D. tank top.

Sincere was from the neighborhood but had done a little time upstate in the past. He knew firsthand how hard life was for the kids in the projects and outside of working for the cable company installing cable, he devoted a large portion of his time doing various things for the youth of the community for that reason. Link and Germ knew him and looked up to him and it was only natural to ask him to coach their team. The kids in the area loved him and looked up to him and he had a supreme gift of gab that made him an excellent motivator. No one could get the results that Sincere did and they knew he'd lead their team to the championship.

Everyone who made the team was introduced to one another. Afterwards Sincere had all the members of the team thoroughly stretch before he started putting them through a series of drills which included shooting from around the court. The way they handled themselves with the ball and the shots they made dictated what position the coach would pick for the players. Sincere loved the way Paul ran the ball, how he was nailing the majority of his shots from all over the court and how he took charge, so he made him a point guard.

Paul was several years younger and a few inches shorter than the other guys since he only stood five foot eight and weighed one hundred forty five pounds. However, he more than made up for his smaller size and frame with the heart he played with. Sincere recognized that Paul didn't display an ounce of fear for any opponent on the court and admired that in him. Paul was equally impressed with Sincere's knowledge of the game and how rock solid diesel he was. His muscles bulged through his tank top and though he was older, as he ran up and down the court directing the players, he never showed any sign of exertion. He knew if anyone messed with their team they'd have quite the fight on their hands.

The practice lasted for about two hours. They made sure to schedule the practices at just before dusk to allow Sincere to get off from work and also because it would be cooler than earlier in the day during summer's sweltering heat. They practiced every other day for two weeks including weekends prior to their first game. By then the team had started to mesh and had become accustomed to each other's style of play. God Sincere stressed the importance of teamwork and told them that teamwork is what makes their dreams work. He informed them that how their performance looked in practice is how it would look during a real game. Their first game was against a squad Alex from Rosenberg Village had thrown together to represent his complex.

The teams consisted of kids between the ages of thirteen to seventeen, but Alex had a few eighteen year old ringers up his sleeve anyway. The game was supposed to be just a friendly competition between the two complexes. Link and Germ both even made a very rare public appearance in the projects and had courtside seats for the game. They knew perfectly well Donnell didn't like Alex for one reason or another and had instructed him not to cause any problems. They kept him within arm's reach just to make sure.

Donnell agreed not to cause any trouble while they were there on his home turf, but that didn't mean that he had to like any of those "saditty co-op niggas" as he called them. Quiet as kept Alex was one of The Family's most dependable and large wholesale cocaine customers. For that reason alone, even if they weren't also there to enjoy what would probably be a great game, they didn't want Donnell or any of their other goons to start any nonsense with Alex or his people. They didn't want anyone causing static with a guy who bought at least ten kilos of coke every week.

Beefing over some petty bullshit could cost them them one hundred and fifty grand he spent with them almost every week. Not to mention that they had also wagered twenty five thousand dollars on the game. The family's business dealings involved many delicate intricacies and politics. The low level members and other soldiers knew nothing of them nor could they ever understand the upper echelon of criminology.

The game got under way and from the beginning the Rosenberg Village team was on top of their A game. Both teams played hard and the energy on the court was intense but they outscored the Bedell squad time and again capitalizing on them turning over the ball repeatedly. At half time, the Rosenberg squad was up by fifteen points. Alex stood there courtside next to his ringers and coach smirking as he peeped from under the dark sunglasses he was wearing. Even though it was now eight thirty at night and pitch black outside. He felt confident that the twenty five grand that he'd bet was all but in the bag.

Courtside was packed. Several of the coaches from the other teams in the league had showed up checking out their opposition. Other high rollers that bet on the tournaments were there and the nicest ball players in the borough showed up to watch the rival factions battle it out on the court as well. There were pretty girls everywhere, dressed to impress and every player had his own cheerleading squad in their midst. Even the cops stood along the gate watching intently instead of patrolling.

The second half of the game started and Paul got in the game. He was nervous and not playing his best at first, but then he remembered how Sincere stressed how team work would be a major factor in the second half because of the way he handled the ball. He stopped focusing on scoring and made it his goal to get the ball down the court to other players who were in better range to make the proper shot. He did so well with the assists that the coach from Alex's team changed his defense strategy and had the taller guys from his squad double team him. Sincere called a time out.

"You playing excellent team ball. However, for us to win the game, you have to pull up and make some big shots." He said to Paul in the huddle. His other teammates wiped sweat from their brows and nodded, giving him encouragement.

"Don't let these guys intimidate you with their size. You got to get out there and play with the same heart that you play with in practice. You show me how big your heart is and I see it...only now you got to get out there and show them. Just relax and work the fundamentals the same way you do in practice. Do the same things here... shake and bake them then stop and pop! Don't be scared of these guys I been watching them and compared to us their game is chump! Now get out there and show these chumps what you got!" Sincere told him with a pat on the head before Paul went charging back into the game.

With Sincere's motivation fresh in Paul's mind, he felt totally unstoppable. The ball was in bounded to the Bedell team and they immediately got it to Paul just as they were instructed to do by their coach. Paul also did as he was told to perfection. He pump faked left and right and began hitting shots repeatedly. Everyone watching now stood to watch. Paul was all over the court and it was his game. He had a double double, ten assists and eleven points by the time the third quarter was over.

The Rosenberg squad started to get nervous because even with them double teaming Paul they weren't able to contain him. They began hacking Paul which sent him to the foul line repeatedly. By the last three minutes of the game, Bedell was now only trailing by four points. The game was more intense and fast paced than some professional broadcast games. One of the kids from Bedell hit a two pointer and everyone was on the edge of their seats. Rosenberg had lost their huge lead and now the score was 79 to 81 with only thirty seconds left in the game according to the digital game clock Link and Germ had put up.

The Rosenberg crew missed the last shot they took and there was a squabble for the ball by both teams when with only nine seconds left and the center for the Bedell squad came up with the ball. He lobbed it to Paul who was in position at half court. With four large steps and only four seconds on the clock, he found himself at the top of the key just beyond the three point line. He stopped and got the shot off just as game ending horn was being blown. Just as he practiced everyday at the park Paul hit the game winning three pointer defeating their opponents by only one point. The park erupted. There was cheering and girls screaming and jumping as Paul hit the shot, as well as heated talk amongst the betters, working out the finals in the small circles.

The coach from Rosenberg's squad protested the shot saying that Paul didn't get the shot off before the sounding of the horn, which caused a group of kids from Rosenberg and Bedell to rush the center court. As the coach argued, the trash talking back and forth started amongst the kids and a tall kid from circle five in Rosenberg got into Sherman's face, beefing. As Sherman and the kid who was almost a foot taller than him were arguing, Duane came jumping up out of nowhere to deliver a devastating right hook to his left eye. The taller kid was dazed and floored by the sneak attack.

That set off a free for all that lasted about five minutes before the adults on hand could quell the volatile situation. Chairs from the side line were being thrown, kids were hit with bottles of soda, and it became a melee. Before police could rush the park, the coaches of both teams as well as Alex himself grabbed the main perpetrators and broke up the fracas. When the smoke cleared Alex told his team that it was time to leave, and that he agreed with the ref's call that the ball did leave Paul's hand before the last horn sounded.

Alex was vexed because his team lost and the fact that it was only by one point added insult to injury. He decided to stand tall as a man and honor the wager that he made with Link and Germ. He walked over to where they were standing and had one of his associates bring him a black knapsack which contained the twenty five thousand dollars that they bet. He shook hands with them after he passed them the money and made his way to his drop- top cherry red 525i BMW. The loss really didn't affect Alex but so much. He grossed over three hundred thousand a week in his complex and the surrounding vicinity so it wasn't a big deal money wise but he'd wanted the win.

After everyone from Rosenberg left the court Donnell gave Duane props for hitting the kid who was in Sherman's face. However, Sincere pulled Duane away from everyone else by his arm and let him have a piece of his mind.

"Yo little man…what the fuck is wrong with you? Why you did some sucka shit like that when two grown ass men was standing there arguing? You really need to slow up for a minute and get wise! Your brother did damn good out there. Why couldn't you just let him have his shine for a minute, huh? See- I know your type. I seen plenty dudes like you get hurt real bad…sometimes killed up north when I was in the pen. Cats like you come to jail with your chest all puffed out, mighty like a lion. Then they come across real killers and end up in the corner quiet as a fuckin' church mouse. There's a lot going on out here in these streets that's way deeper than fun and games!" Sincere's reprimanding left Duane feeling an inch tall.

He just stood there in shock, not quite knowing what to say. He thought Sincere would be singing him praise like Donnell for what he'd done. Normally the only adult to speak to him like that was his father, and Jean hadn't done that in quite some time. Duane stood there stuttering totally at a loss for words.

His shoulders slumped then Sincere took it on a different track. He wasn't trying to demoralize, he wanted to teach. "I can't lie though little man, you do have a vicious right hook though…you know how to box?" Sincere asked.

"Nah." Duane said shaking his head which was still hanging. He took it to heart that Sincere said he'd done some "sucka shit".

"You want to learn?"

"I already can rumble…you said you saw the way I socked that cat and almost knocked him out?" Duane asked. He tried to pipe up some pride for his actions that started the melee on the court. Sincere let out a sarcastic chuckle then responded, "What I saw was a young guy trying to steal the spotlight from the exact copy of himself by sucker punching another kid while he was off guard. If you want to impress me let me see you in the ring with that cat, one on one with his hands up! Son, don't you realize your brother's success is your success and vice versa? If you want to see yourself without looking in the mirror all you have to do is look in your brother's face. See the reason you acting that way is because you hate yourself."

"What?" Duane yelled, smoothing his fresh clothes. "You sound crazy man! Who you think you are to be grabbing all on me talking all that mumbo jumbo?"

He had never heard anything so ridiculous. He was the man. He had the fly gear, a pretty girl on his arm, props cause he was down with The Family and a Honda Elite scooter that everyone stared at when he rode through. He had it going on and he had no reason to hate himself.

"I'm responsible for all of you in my midst whether you behave like an ignoramus or act civilized. You got to realize you are your brother, and your brother is you. Any way son...there's two type of men in this world. The ones who fight and the ones who box. You have to make up your mind as to what type of man you want to be in life. Are you a fighting man or a boxing man?"

"I'm a fighter...why what's the difference?" Duane shot back defiantly.

"Because when you look at me you see a boxer...a boxer for real. Know and understand that intelligence controls all things. You box with your mind, and you fight with your heart. There's a world of difference between the two types of men. Yes a boxing man uses his mind and still has to have the heart to fight. The boxing man has to have the intelligence to know which blows to take and which ones he should slip also! Now let me ask you one last time...do you want to learn how to box, yes or no?" Sincere had an authority and powerful magnetism that made Duane fall back. He looked up to him too and he was wise enough to know the older brother was gracing him with a life jewel.

"Yes…I guess so."

"That's peace, young blood, because I also teach young men to box as well. I teach the boxing class on the days we don't have games or practice. Always remember a man answers a question straight to the point. You got to raider that 'I guess so' shit. Meet me tomorrow at seven in the community center right over by 118-12. As a matter of fact bring your peoples with you too if you want." Sincere gave Duane a smile and a playful smack on his head, then dismissed him back in the general direction of Donnell and his crew.

What Duane didn't know is that God Sincere was a Golden Glove winner that qualified for the 1976 U.S. Olympic boxing team. However, on his assent to glory he got derailed running the streets with no direction because he didn't have a job or the means to care for himself legitimately. He ended up robbing banks and doing seven years hard time in Attica with three years of parole hanging over his head. He'd only been home a few years and dedicated much of his time giving local knuckle heads like Duane a decent shot in life by providing counsel to them.

Sincere was a full grown man with regrets about some things in his past. Yet he was still grateful for being young enough to have a second chance to make something out of his life. He showed zeal and gratitude for his new lease on life by educating the youth and being the father figure for them that he lacked as a youth. He liked being around young people because it kept him young and brand new.

That night when the twins got home they delivered the news to their parents about how Paul was the deciding factor in his team winning the game as well as how Duane would be taking up boxing. Once again, Jean and Winsome were ecstatic about the news their sons were bringing home. Winsome expressed some concern about Duane possibly getting hurt boxing but Jean thought it would be good for him. It would help him channel his energy and give him something constructive to do with his time while he wasn't working at the family's restaurant. That all suited Duane just fine because now he would have a legitimate reason to spend so much time in the projects outside of just saying he wanted to see Paul play basketball.

The very next day Duane went over to his Aunt Gwen's house while she was preparing to work a shift at their family's restaurant. She was waiting for her new and much younger lover named Gordon whom she'd recently started seeing. Hell, China wasn't the only one who could get someone else or so she thought to herself. Gwen and her daughter Dorrine made their way toward Gordon's car once he pulled up to the curb ready to take them both to the restaurant.

Shortly afterwards, Duane and P.J. made their way to the community center in the projects. Sincere was already there preparing a group of about a dozen youngsters for drills he had them all do. He made both Duane and P.J. put on gloves and the proper required pads before they all started hitting the heavy bag, jumping rope, and jabbing the hitting mitts he wore on his hands while moving them invarious positions.

Sincere got all the boys familiar with one another through out their workout. Most of the teenaged guys were already familiar with Duane because of his affiliation with The Family. After about two hours of learning some fundamental skills in the ring and jogging, Duane had to get P.J. back home. By the time they were done that evening Duane felt as if his arms were going to fall off. He didn't stick around the projects too long because he still didn't want P.J. to know just exactly what he did while hanging out there. However, it was cool that he had another steady activity to do with his little cousin because now they could spend more time together.

This way maybe P.J. may be able to get his mind off being depressed about his parents breaking up and his mother seeing another man besides his father. The day went by without a problem. Since there were a number of shootings and unsolved homicides on the back blocks, the 131st precinct had their hands full and weren't as concerned with running through the buildings for the time being. The following day when Paul attended practice he noticed a group of girls sitting on the benches. They were cute and they seemed to be watching Paul's every move.

Since hitting the game winning shot against Rosenberg Village, Paul had become a star amongst the young ladies. After practice, he went to the water fountain between where the handball courts and benches were right where all the girls were. They all were appealing to him but the one who stood out the most was eating an orange push up pop. Not only did she stand out to him she seemed to be staring at him or at least expressing the same amount of interest in him as he was in her. There just seemed to be an intense magnetic vibe they both felt instinctively.

"Hi my name …" Is all Paul could say before he was swiftly interrupted.

"I know you…we all know who you are! You're Shake and Bake. You won the game for us the other night against Rosenberg. My name is Raina." She smiled, not the least bit shy. "You wanna go and hang out or something?" Her straightforward manner caught Paul by surprise and totally off guard. He wasn't used yet to his overnight celebrity status.

He played it off as best as he could. "Ye…yyy…. yeah give me your number and I'll call you so we can set something up."

The two of them exchanged numbers and began a whirlwind teenage love affair.

Paul was still shy and didn't have much experience with females but something about Raina made him feel at ease and he was totally comfortable around her. The two would spend the next couple of weeks talking on the phone late nights getting to know one another and just shooting the breeze. He found out that she was of mixed heritages, half black and Puerto Rican. That explained her last name being Estrada and her long shoulder length wavy jet black locks. She stood about five foot six and was a size seven dress with dangerous curves that had grown men noticing her. Even though she was sixteen and older than Paul she liked him and wasn't shy about her attraction to him.

Their first official date was with the rest of the members of the team to Rye Play Land up in Westchester County. For their winning several games in a row, Link and Germ chartered three busses to take members of the basketball team and Sincere's boxing squad there for a day of fun. The park was about thirty minutes north of the Bronx and was a well known destination for summertime shenanigans the whole family could enjoy. The chartered busses also had other neighborhood people along to share in the festivities.

Even the old people, who generally hated the drug dealers and blamed them for the ruin and degradation crack heads visited on the community even more than they blamed the crackheads came along. The old ladies from the various Tenant Patrols and Block Associations put their anger with the young boys aside for one day and there was caravan of cars containing the who's who and royalty of the Bedell Houses following the chartered busses. There was much love amongst everyone who came up on the chartered busses. Everyone was having such a good time and actually behaving themselves as a real family.

Paul and Raina spent the day together holding hands as they rode various rides and played different games. Duane could have also brought Kiesha but decided to see if he could meet some other girls there on the side. Raina took Paul by the hand and led him back to the bus they came in about a half hour before they were scheduled to leave that evening.

They snuck and sat right back where they were sitting on their way up state to the park. Raina took a windbreaker from out of her bag that she was carrying and placed it over her then grabbed Paul's hand and placed it on her chest. She grabbed Paul's head from behind and began kissing him. Paul went absolutely mad he thought his pants were on fire! He'd kissed a couple of girls before however not quite like this. Never had he really felt a girl's breast before let alone while they tongue kissed.

Raina placed one of Paul's hands down her pants and pulled his head in the general direction of her chest. Paul couldn't believe what was happening he was totally in shock.He tried to keep his composure but he simply couldn't he never thought that he'd be losing his virginity to a girl who was so beautiful. Paul's little man was harder than Chinese arithmetic and he was practically drooling at the mouth when all of a sudden the unthinkable happened!

He couldn't hold it back Paul began slightly jerking around in his seat groaning as he felt the muscles in his thighs and lower stomach go numb as his face also began to tighten. With all the excitement going on Paul prematurely ejaculated in his pants. He was beyond embarrassed and Raina figured out what happened. She didn't want to embarrass her boyfriend any farther so she decided to go to the bathroom on the back of the bus to get herself together.

It was a good thing for Paul that he was wearing dark blue jeans or everyone who was on the bus would have known about his little accident. When Raina came back Paul took his turn in the bathroom washing up. It wasn't a second too soon either the driver of the bus opened the door and started letting everyone else onto the bus. Duane and P.J. were amongst the first to get on the bus and they saw Paul and Raina sitting next to each other holding hands making goo goo eyes at one another. Raina's wind breaker was still over Paul's lap and Duane saw that his brother had a certain twinkle in his eyes that he didn't have on the way to the park. Duane didn't say anything to put Paul on the spot he just nodded his head and shot him an all knowing yet wicked grin.

After they got back to Queens it only took a few days for Paul and Raina to arrange and execute their first full blown sexual encounter. It would have been sooner, but Jean had been sick with hay fever for a couple of days and he missed work. Finally, when Paul knew Jean and Winsome would both be at work he invited Raina over to his house and they went at it all day long. In fact Paul liked it so much they did it several times that day. When they were done Paul walked his sweet heart to the Q4A bus stop and saw her on her way.

Paul was so drained he called Sincere to tell him he didn't feel good and that he would be missing practice that day. When Paul knew that his parents weren't going to be home and Raina had some free time he'd invite her over for what became their favorite festivity that summer. It got so bad that Paul started missing so many practices and not properly contributing in games they way he had done throughout the season that Sincere had to bench him.

That was a wakeup call for him. He'd fallen madly in love and was smitten as was Raina but he also knew he needed the practice on the court because school time was rapidly approaching and he wanted his former shine back. He told Raina that they would have to take a break or at least cut back on seeing each other as much every week. He also requested that she not come to a few of his games at least until he got his head back on straight.

She was angry and hurt and couldn't understand when he said it was because of the impact on his game but she backed off. In a matter of two weeks after making all his practices and showing Sincere improvement, he was once again allowed to be a starting player. Outside of that, the summer was filled with Duane and his crew going on trips. They went to Hershey Park, Rye Playland a few more times and Coney Island in Brooklyn.

When they weren't going on trips hanging out and hustling in the projects, their favorite place to be seen was at the local roller rink known as City skates. Friday and Saturday nights brought out all the prettiest girls from the whole borough and they had quite a good time there mixing and mingling, even when they didn't skate. That summer was indeed magical time and a transition point for The Family and Duane's young crew as well.

CHAPTER EIGHT

By the time September rolled around, the basketball league was coming to a close and it was time for school to start. The Bedell team had won the championship for their league and had earned Link as well as Germ over a quarter of a million dollars in betting revenue. Part of it was for winning the games while the rest came from side bets about who would or wouldn't make shots while the game was in progress. Sincere still trained the boys and out of gratitude the Family gave him funding for equipment he needed for the kids he would train.

Duane ended up surprising everyone and getting into Brooklyn Technical high school on DeKalb Avenue in the Fort Green section of Brooklyn. Even though he ran the streets he was still supremely intelligent and he'd aced the specialized test. Paul ended up attending Andrew Jackson high school while both Kiesha and Raina attended August Martin with Junior and Terry. By this time Sherman was a full time hustler but would still hang out around the schools his friends attended to show off after dropping out himself.

Duane absolutely loved going to school in Brooklyn. He loved getting out of Queens and seeing how people operated in Brooklyn and other boroughs of the city. Sometimes he'd take the train straight through Brooklyn to school then there'd be times where he took the train through Manhattan to school for a change in scenery. Brooklyn Tech was a giant melting pot of four thousand smart kids from all over the city and different backgrounds. There were even some students of West Indian decent there as well and overall he felt as if he had more in common with kids there than at his former school.

For the first time in his life he had his own separate identity from his brother. Some people who knew Paul from the playgrounds of Jamaica called him Shake which was short for his newly earned title of Shake and Bake. He was working hard to earn a starting position on Andrew Jackson's basketball squad. He saw action in a couple of Junior varsity games and actually ended up being a major contributor with three assists.

Everything was going fine for the boys and their little crew. After school Duane and P.J. still went to train with Sincere. Duane still had his position in the projects too and was so well liked by Donnell that he started giving Duane packages to run here and there to earn a little extra money. All was well up until the spring of 1987 when two kids who were bigger than Duane attempted to rob him for his glasses and the small chain that he was wearing.

It happened right on DeKalb Ave, only about three blocks away from his school. The one guy looked to be about seventeen and had a grimace on his dark skinned face. He stood about six feet tall weighing what seemed to be two hundred pounds as far as Duane could tell. The other guy was brown skinned one stood about six feet tall as well but weighed much less than his partner in crime. He was much skinnier than his accomplice.

"That's a nice pair of frames paw…how much they run you yo'?" The dark skinned guy asked approaching Duane with the skinny one in tow about a yard or so in back of him. Duane already knew the reputation Brooklyn had for stick up's. He'd been told by Sincere, Donnell and others that if someone pulled out a gun or knife on him and he wasn't armed to just get a good look at their face and they'd get them later on.

They warned him not to play the hero role going to school in Brooklyn so far away from his home turf all alone. At first, Duane thought that he was just being paranoid about getting robbed. He kept walking right along DeKalb Ave. toward the train station. Then after he got a quarter of the way down the block the dark skinned guy forcefully asked "Yo my man, don't you hear me talkin' to you…I said how much you paid for those glasses?" His partner in crime was by his side blocking Duane from walking down the block. Thinking of a good response all Duane could come up with was…

"An arm and a leg!"   He stated with obvious distain for the simple minded question and the guy who was asking it.

"Oh Shorty you think you a hard rock huh… so tell me this smart ass…what you gonna do for that chain and them frames?"

They surrounded him, making no bones about the fact that they meant to rob him. Duane looked at the skinny dude and knew since he couldn't fight, he probably had a weapon.

"Come on man hurry up and take Shorty shit so we can break out!"

Duane noticed that as the guy who was lunged toward him motioning as if he were about to pop his chain from around his neck didn't have a weapon and it was on! Duane had been training with Sincere all summer and in fact he'd become one of Sincere's star pupils. The God Sincere taught Duane a fighting style called fifty two hand blocks that if used properly was deadly. Sincere learned and perfected this fighting style in the penitentiary.

He leaned this style of fighting to fight off the blows of corrections officer's night sticks. The better you were at the style the more c.o.'s you could fight off. Sincere was a true master at it and could fight off the best riot squads or "Turtles" as they were known because of all their shields and protective clothing. Anyone who could fight and knew this style of warfare in the street was a menace to a guy with sub-par or average hand skills.

He made up his mind right there on the spot to severely punish both of them. In a flash, Duane side stepped the brown skinned guy and blocked the arm he was reaching for his chain with. The guy made another lunge for Duane right as Duane caught him with a two piece combination to his right eye and to his mouth.

The tall brown skinned kid was shocked that Duane had the heart; much less the skills and speed to not only block him but to hit him and catch him nice enough to bust his lip. In a blind rage, the tall brown skinned guy drew back his right arm and balled up his fist and tried to hit Duane but was unsuccessful. Duane was able to block all the blows the guy threw with acute precision and backhanded him with a fist to his temple. The back hand gave Duane the leverage he needed to instantly knock out the would- be strong arm robber when he came close enough.

All summer long Duane studied pressure points while he learned the sweet science of pugilism from Sincere. He remembered that Sincere kept drilling him letting him know that it only took five pounds of pressure to completely knock a man out. Indeed that was one lesson well taught by Sincere and lived out to its fullest capacity on DeKalb Ave. Proof positive was the brown skinned guy who was lying on the ground knocked out twitching and bleeding all over the pavement. The bigger dark skinned guy responded by saying...

"Oh so you really think you a hard rock...well I'm the hardest of them all bring it on chump!"

Then he put his hands up and began to bounce on the balls of his feet as he moved in a circular motion like boxers do when they fight. The dark skinned guy kept talking shit as he bounced around sizing Duane up. Then, all at once Duane swiftly delivered a devastating right jab to the dark skinned guy's nose sending him crashing to the ground in severe agony bleeding profusely from his nostrils. People had started to gather to watch the spectacle and they couldn't believe that Duane had successfully beaten both of the older guys the fuck up. There were kids from Duane's school and the several others nearby that had gathered to watch the three minute spectacle unfold right in front of the pizzeria.

The whole thing didn't mean much to Duane he just figured that these two guys were just some local cats who were looking for an easy victim to rob. They got what they deserved as far as he was concerned. When Duane got on the A train on his way back home to Queens it seemed as if all eyes were on him. People he saw everyday in school and on the train that never spoke to him before were all of a sudden his friend. He paid no mind to any of them, they were "nerds" as far as he was concerned and he didn't want anything to do with any of them, except for the females of course.

A few guys tried to spark up a conversation but he just nodded his head and smiled at them. Then he put on the head phones of his walkman and began blasting his M.C. Shan tape as loud as he could to block them all out. That gesture was his polite way of saying "please get the fuck out of my face." In all it was just a small hassle to Duane but when he got to the projects he had a good laugh about the incident with his crew. He told Sincere and he was proud that Duane had used what he'd taught him in self defense. The whole crew laughed about the incident between making sales and making runs for Donnell.

The next day in school Duane was a certified superstar in the hall ways of Brooklyn Tech, because the word had spread about his fight. It was now solidified that Duane was that kid from Queens who was golden with his hands. He was getting the same treatment that he got in school for knocking these clowns down and out as he did for beating up Steven a few years earlier only now it seemed to be intensified tenfold. However, in his last class of the day, the deans came to speak with Duane with two men in suits. The two men in suits had grimaces on their faces even though they tried their best to seem as though they were really smiling. They asked that Duane go with them to the deans' office so they could have a little talk.

Duane didn't have the slightest idea why he was being taken to the office and who the two men in suits were. When they got there though, he was shocked to see both of the half way thugs who tried to rob him the day before. It turned out the two men in suits were detectives from the 83rd precinct investigating what they were told was an assault the day before. The two guys were students at Westinghouse High only a few blocks away on the other side of Flatbush Avenue.

The detectives said there were a string of incidents where a gang of kids from Brooklyn Tech were harassing and robbing other kids from Westinghouse. The two Westinghouse cats' tale was that Duane just walked up on them at the pizza shop, began to savagely beat them for no apparent reason at all and then robbed them before running into the train station. Duane thought that was so ridiculous that he didn't really mount any defense, going along with the crazy story, expecting the police to tell them to cut it out at any second. He didn't know the detectives were so eager to make a collar and already had a witness that said that it was Duane who had put his hands on both of the other guys.

Even before rolling up at the class to get him, they had already pulled his file. Once the detectives got a hold of the record that Duane had in the Queens County Family Court system and they saw that he had beaten another kid to the point he had to be hospitalized, it was all over for him. That's all the ammunition that they needed to railroad the poor kid into Spotford Youth Detention Center in the Bronx. He was sentenced to a year and booked for assault and battery.

After Duane was sentenced in Kings County (Brooklyn) Family Court, Jean had to catch Winsome as she passed out right there in the courtroom. They led Duane out with a group of other young men who were also sentenced and sent to a van waiting to take them to their destination. On his way out, Winsome came to just in time to see Duane mouth the words I love you to his mother. It warmed Winsome's heart but that just intensified the frequency of tears streaming down her face.

Winsome felt guilty and blamed herself for the predicament that her son was in. She was so proud that Duane was accepted into one of the most prestigious high schools in New York City, but was angry that her son was unjustly incarcerated. She believed her son's story one hundred percent on how that the two guys tried to rob him. She blamed herself for buying her children expensive clothes at such a young age.

It was so ironic to her because she'd overcome so many barriers in America to be successful and wanted her kids to have the best things that she could afford them.Only for the ignorance and greed of others to overwhelm her son or so she thought. If this was the price of success in America Winsome didn't want it for her or her family. She'd be more than happy to give up the small amount of success and personal wealth she and Jean had acquired in America. At that moment all she desired was to have peace of mind and to know that her children could be free and prosper on their own.

After several weeks of blaming herself for her sons fate Winsome made a remark to Mrs. Willcott in the restaurant one morning as they were preparing to open for the day.

"You know Mrs. Willy sometimes Mi wish that we never would of left ah Yard. I really and truly wish Jean didn't have to be so violent in those times that led up to all ah we coming to foreign. Because mi think violence breed more violence I think all our bad luck is some kind of retribution for what happened fi Dexter you know…" Winsome said about to finish her statement when Mrs. Willcott sat her down at the table and told her a family secret that only she knew and was hidden with her for many years.

"Well Winnie…I'm not so sure of that! Mi never could a say nothing before, because you all ready had enough troubles to worry about just trying to make it you know. Now you is established here in this country and I is getting up in age and have a truly serious confession to make to you." By the tone of her voice and the look in her eyes Winsome could tell that whatever Mrs. Willcott was about to reveal had been something that had been tormenting her for quite some time.

"Well…you know how we tell you that your father ah go catch a disease and die when you was a pickney? Your momma…God rest her poor soul, tell me say she knew that your father had some problems with Donovan Vassel and in dem times he was a very powerful and dangerous man. Donovan started working in the mines and wanted your father out of the way so he could run his operation there without any problems. Your momma tell me that Donovan threatened to kill Conroy on different occasions."

"Conroy was well liked and very popular not only at work but also in the community so it would have caused dem a whole heap ah trouble if they would have just shot him. She told me she was sure Donovan himself or one of his men poisoned Conroy and that's what kill him! Donovan had friends at the coroner's office who said he died of cancer from the mines dem but your momma tell me different. So you see chile sometimes violence is good…sometimes ounoo affi even the score seen!" Mrs. Willcott declared in a matter of fact toned voice as she nonchalantly rose from the table and gracefully went in the back to the kitchen.

All Winsome could do in lieu of the devastating revelation Mrs. Willcott had just made was just sit there in total shock and confusion about what she'd just found out. She had to come to grips with the fact that her former lover's father was actually responsible in one way or another for both of her parent's demise. Now everything was all starting to make sense why Dexter's father hated her and Jean so much…it was personal! Now it was dawning on her that by killing Dexter Jean had evened the score for her father's murder.

In all reality Donovan actually wanted to finish what he started by killing her father and wipe out the whole family. However by Conroy having only daughters he figured that he didn't have anything to worry about. He never figured on one of the daughters men having a reason what so ever to come after him or his family. Donovan's treachery and deceit came back on him three hundred sixty degrees in all.

Winsome felt a lot better about hearing how Donovan had his head blown clean off his shoulders in his own home now. She knew more than ever that he deserved every bit of the flames and buckshot from Bashir's shotgun blast that burned the flesh away from his face. The only regret she had in regard to how he died is that she wished it could have been slower and a lot more painful. She wanted to dig Donovan up and kill him again her damn self.

She wanted that son of a bitch to R.I.P. (Rot in Piss) for all eternity. She felt so sorry for her poor mother now knowing that there was nothing she could have done to warn her about Dexter's powerful family. If they would have found out they would have also killed her and Winsome without a second thought. Her mother lived her life in constant fear that at any moment the Vassels would eventually finish what they started. Now Winsome knew the real reason for her mother being executed and why her mother never favored that bastard Dexter…even when he was on his best behavior.

The terrible news that she'd learned from Mrs. Willcott proved to be too much for Winsome to bear in her already fragile mind state. She ended up just waiting for Gwen and a couple of their employees to arrive and decided to take the rest of the day off. She was an absolute wreck and had to go home and console her bitter sweet emotions. She was so sad to find out the true reason of her father Conroy's death yet happy to learn that her son's situation wasn't caused by some sort of curse brought on by Jean's actions. Winsome rarely drank however on this occasion, she decided having a couple of glasses of white wine and taking a long hot bubble bath before she turned in and crawled under the cover in her bed was the only way to get through this.

Meanwhile in Spotford, Duane had a fight at least once a week for the first couple of months he was there. Sometimes he would win, sometimes he would lose but all in all his opponent would never get the best of him. He never backed down from a confrontation the whole time that he was locked up. That's all that mattered to Duane more than winning or losing...respect.

He wanted to be respected no matter what under any circumstance. He prided himself on the fact that no one throughout that whole facility, whether it was an inmate or a corrections officer, could say that they chumped him. Most of the time people who are bullies look for people who will give them the least amount of resistance to victimize. Duane was fully aware of this mindset and wanted to be known and remembered as a warrior, not a victim.

Duane made a couple of friends and clicked up with a few Brooklyn guys out of Brownsville and East New York. Once people saw that Duane had a crew to back him up and the fact that they already knew that he was a brawler caused most of the problems that he was having with others to cease. Duane kept himself busy by writing letters to Kiesha and with visits from his family. The year that he'd received was actually reduced to eight months city time.

Duane had never been away from his family for so long but the actual eight months that he ended up doing wasn't as bad for him as other kids who didn't have anyone to support them during their time away. By the time Duane came home it was 1988 and he had earned a new nick name. He loved Big Daddy Kane's song "Raw" so much that he'd always recite the words as he performed his daily chores. Plus the fact that he had so much heart and was a brawler his new crew from Brooklyn dubbed him Raw.

He touched back down in Queens in late January of that year and the protocol had drastically changed in the projects by that time. Terry was now working in 118-14 New York Boulevard selling jumbos of crack hand to hand as a member of Donnell's crew. Donnell promoted him when one of his other younger soldiers he had in that position got knocked by the police. Junior was also working in the same building as well as a runner who got money from customers who wanted large sums of drugs. He'd take their money and then in turn bring the desired amount of drugs without revealing where they were stashed.

Donnell was still giving orders and in control of dishing out the product to the workers already for distribution. He was in charge of keeping order of the majority of The Family's business affairs in the projects as well. From the moment Duane saw Donnell again he could tell that Donnell was doing big things with The Family. Big D was now driving a spanking new jet black 190 Mercedes Benz and had given his baby blue Jetta to his little cousin Sherman. The days of riding those scooters had long faded away for Sherman. At the tender age of sixteen and driving a foreign car by the standards of the hood, Shiz was that dude!

Duane ended up getting back in tune with his old partner in crime and Shiz put him on to a whole different caper that he was now running. Sherman rarely sold anything in the projects now even though he still lived there. For his sixteenth birthday, Donnell gave him his kitted up baby blue Jetta and his own spot to run in a private house on Sutton Boulevard. Sherman's new spot made about thirty thousand dollars a week. The majority of the money would have to be turned over to Donnell who in turn would have to give his superiors a cut.

It didn't matter much to Shiz that he had to turn over approximately $25,000.00 of the $30,000.00 weekly take. After he paid his workers he still was making $3.000.00 a week at sixteen. All that mattered to him was that he had the status of a boss where as though he could put on who he wanted and that he was running his own spot. Shiz personally netted $144,000.00 from this one location annually. Duane had always been his right hand man so it was only right that he put him on with his new operation. Terry and Junior were cool but they already were doing just fine over in 118-14.

He wanted to show Duane some love so he could not only get on his feet but elevate himself as well. Plus Sutton Boulevard could get rough at times and Shiz knew that Duane could fight and he had heart. Now that he ran his own spot and was responsible for so much money, things were much more serious. Thus his level of defense and attack had also elevated. Shiz had a small cache of weapons and was armed with a Jet black double action sixteen shot Beretta at all times now and he just knew Duane would love that.

One day after Duane had been back home for only about a week, Shiz waited until it got good and dark to collect the days earnings from his workers and leave for the day. Afterwards he and Duane went to an isolated area in Bedell Park near where its large pond was and Shiz passed him a Beretta and told him to fire it. The gun was a lot heavier than he'd thought it would be and it definitely wasn't as easy to handle as people on T.V. made it seem.

Duane took a few moments to get used to the weight of the gun then found a trash can near a street lamp clear on the other side of the pond to aim at. He then proceeded to let off a volley of a half a dozen shots in its general direction hitting it about three times in the process. At that precise moment Duane fell head over heels in love with the power he felt when he held those precious four and a half ponds of steel in his hands. Sherman gave him a tip, he told him to close one eye and hold his breath when aiming at targets that were more than a hundred feet away from him.

All of what Shiz was teaching Duane as if he were a pro at the gun range he'd learned from Donnell when Duane was locked up. The very next time he fired at the trash can he did exactly what Shiz told him to do and hit the trash can with every shot he fired. When they were done target practicing Shiz passed the Beretta and two magazines of ammo filled to the top with dumb-dumb rounds and told him it was his now that he knew how to shoot it. Duane thanked Shiz and walked with his chest poked out a little now as they made their way to the car so they wouldn't get booked for the gun that Duane had fired at least a dozen times.

As the weeks went by, Duane started hanging out more and more back in the projects with Junior and even Terry on some occasions. However being with Shiz on Sutton had become a constant thing especially now since they were handling their business there. Duane's new role was that of an enforcer. If any customers got too unruly Duane would personally escort them off of their block and if they were really really unruly, he'd do it at gun point. If one of the guys who were making runs for Shiz messed up any money or if they even slightly disrespected Shiz they'd find themselves pistol whipped immediately by Duane's gun.

If there were any problems that arose Duane was the first one to swiftly address it and Shiz rewarded him handsomely for his deeds. After about three months of Duane putting all of Sherman's workers in the house and on the block under extreme pressure and fear for life and limb, productivity grew an extra ninety percent. That meant some of the guys were skimming from the top before because the profits grew from thirty thousand to fifty thousand a week now. None of them wanted to trifle with Duane because in doing so you'd be gambling with your life. Shiz and Duane became so tight after he'd scared all of the workers straight that the operation on Sutton was no longer a one man show. They both ran it after a while.

Even though they were both still technically adolescents Duane handled all his affairs in regard to their operation as effectively and efficiently as if he were a thirty year old man. Duane was built to be a boss. He had a certain air and presence about him that exceeded his chronological age. Three months in the lifestyle that they were involved in especially on the level they were on was the equivalent to a whole year in the average person's life. Duane and his associates were far from living an average square life, speeding at the rate of a mile a minute, flying by the seat of their pants. Thus after being involved in the drug game for the better part of three years Duane and company were aging at the rate of four years socially and mentally in the span of one year.

Their operation was solid and the money was flowing lovely. Whenever the two of them went shopping or hanging out on Jamaica Avenue they were like movie stars in the streets of Queens. Girls would stop and point before they fell over themselves just to speak to either Duane or Sherman. Their hot spot was especially in the Coliseum Mall on 165th St. They had a habit of shopping for gold chains there at least once a week even though Duane would have to hide his jewelry or leave it with Terry or Sherman when he was finished hustling.

There was no shortage of females to choose from either. Even though Duane and his sweetheart Kiesha were still officially an item both Duane and Sherman had more top shelf females than either one of them could count on their hands and feet combined. Some were in their age group but most of them were grown ass women at least five years their senior. That didn't matter to the women that they kept company with all that mattered to them was that they "had it going on". But all their fun and games came to an abrupt halt toward the end of the summer that same year.

Sherman and Duane caught up to one of their workers a really light skinned kid named Kahlik who owed them five thousand dollars for over three weeks. He wasn't where he'd usually be and he appeared to be ducking them. They spotted him one day as Shiz and Duane were cruising down Finch Boulevard on Duane's old block. Duane hopped out of the car and immediately began to beat Kahlik on sight with not a word being said or question being asked.

As Duane punched him over and over again, he tried to cop a plea and put his hands up to show he wasn't going to fight but eventually just dropped and balled up in a fetal position when it became apparent Duane didn't want any excuses or explanations. He was laying there balled up and begging for mercy when Duane heard sirens.

While he had the now whimpering and moaning debtor on the ground, an unmarked police cruiser had come upon the scene and two plainclothes officers jumped out, weapons drawn to stop the fracas.

"Freeze! Lemme see your hands, motherfucker!" One cop screamed as they approached Duane. They saw that he was armed when he raised his hands and his t-shirt came up and revealed the butt of his gun. They violently tackled Duane to the ground and retrieved the gun before he could make a move and immediately began to handcuff him. Afterwards they approached Sherman and asked him if he was with Duane or not.

"Hell no, I don't know this cat or why he's beating that pussy the fuck up!" Sherman stated emphatically, not wanting a beef with the police. They asked the victim if he knew whether Sherman or Duane knew one another and if he knew either of them.

"N...na....No, officer!" Kahlik responded whimpering like the bitch he was with a bruised and battered face after Duane gave him the all telling stare of death. Fearing for his life the worker told the police he had a misunderstanding with Duane over a hard look between the two. The cops knew better but all they could do was try and encourage him to snitch.

"Do you wanna press charges?" One of the officers probed.

"Ah...nah man. I just had to learn not to be staring at people in a funny way no more. I'll be fine." Kahlik said knowing what would happen if he gave any information to the police. Knowing that they already had a righteous collar, the plainclothes cops settled for the story. Even though they knew it was a crock of shit.

"Here take this card my name is Officer Hinds call me at that number on the card if you change your mind, son." One said, giving Khalik a card while looking at Duane and then Sherman.

They searched Sherman's car and couldn't find anything to hold him on so they had to let him go. However as for Duane, they had him cold on the gun alone and there was no way he could get out of being busted red handed with it. On their way to the precinct, the short husky officer in the passenger seat who was wearing a Mets hat identified himself as officer Hinds. He instructed his partner to pull over to the side of the street only a few blocks away from the station house. He told Duane that they were going to have a little talk before he took him into the station

"O.K. partner...you're in a whole lot of trouble... you do know that right?" The officer started. Duane gave him a blank look as if he didn't even speak English. He spoke in the same slow and methodical tone to make his words have more effect psychologically.

"Let me explain to you just how this works. You see me? I'm a nice guy. I don't want to be an asshole. So if you be nice to me, I'll be nice to you and we'll see if we can knock some time off your sentence. I'll tell the D.A. that you co-operated with our investigation.

So what do you say pal…you think you can handle that? I mean come on, I think that's more than fair and it's simple enough. All I need to know is where you got this gun and if you can tell us about any of all these homicides that's been happening in this area lately. So what's it gonna be pal?" The short husky white middle aged officer said trying to butter Duane up.

"I don't know jack shit about no guns or no bodies. Y'all got me. Now do what you do? I'm not doing no police work for you and I ain't sayin' nothing until I can talk to a lawyer!" Duane stated vehemently.

"Oh so you wanna be a wise ass, huh? You're gonna say some more before you see a lawyer whether you like it or not…believe you me!" The cop instructed his partner to drive down an isolated back block down Claude Ave off of New York Boulevard. Once they reached their desired destination the same officer who was just speaking so nice to Duane, trying to broker a deal with him took a metal night stick from the front of the unmarked car they were driving. He opened the back door then began beating Duane in his thighs and poking him in his stomach and ribs. Hinds also began beating him in the upper torso around the chest and arm area as not to leave any visible bruises.

"How's that feel, son...you alright...you alright? Bet you wanna talk real nice now, huh...I bet you don't wanna treat me like friggin' a jag off any more, do you? So come on, talk...who has the guns out here?" Officer Hinds demanded.

Duane just lay in the back seat of the cruiser in extreme pain knowing that giving up any information to the authorities was an automatic death sentence in the street and especially in jail. Even though he was only locked in a juvenile facility he saw firsthand how snitches were dealt with in the penile system. He'd much rather take his chances with the judge and police instead. Being judged by twelve people was much better than being laid to rest by six pallbearers any day. He lay in the back seat in great agony almost unconscious from the officer's assault while Hinds stood over him taunting him. Although he was on the brink of passing out somehow Duane got the courage and strength to hiss a flippant remark through his clenched teeth. "Fuck you pussy...you hit like a little girl!" Hinds lost it and was without a doubt going to crack Duane's skull wide open until his partner got out the car and stopped him.

"Aww come on, Tony chill out...let's get him to the station, this friggin' egg plant ain't gonna talk. You gotta give him some credit for the size of the balls he's got on him. Most of the homeboys would have pissed their pants by now. Besides, if he throws up like the last one, I ain't cleaning up his guts off the floor this time."

Hinds reluctantly agreed, giving Duane the stink eye as they drove him to the 131st precinct to process him. Being as though he had just been out of jail for a little over eight months and was on probation he didn't want to give the police his real name but had to so they could contact his parents since he was still a minor. The authorities didn't get in contact with Duane's parents until later that evening. When Jean got the call about his boy all he could do was shake his head in disappointment and think back to all the times he used to beat Duane and all the talks he had with him. Jean took a pause and questioned himself as a parent. In his heart of hearts he wondered exactly where he went wrong.

Even though Jean didn't want to tell his wife what happened to their son he had to because he knew that she would worry herself sick if she didn't hear from him that night. Ever since Duane was locked up in Brooklyn, Winsome was constantly on edge about both her sons' welfare. Jean came in the living room and made sure that Winsome was sitting down before he delivered the bad news to her. Once she heard that Duane was locked up for a gun possession beef she went ballistic, screaming and crying from the massive disappointment she felt in Duane.

Being as though the authorities didn't get in contact with Duane's parents until later in the evening, they couldn't take him to central booking for his arraignment until the next morning. That meant he'd miss night court and would have to spend the night in the 131st precinct because the Queens central booking facility was packed to capacity that humid summer night. He was arraigned the next morning at eleven A.M.

Winsome got Gwen to call Mr. Silverman, their former employer who had become a minor celebrity for successfully defending mobsters, to represent Duane in court. The entire family sat in the second row behind some defendants who were with their lawyers. A few of them were also chained and escorted into the courtroom by detectives. They bought Duane from the back and announced his case.

"Next docket up on the calendar!" The judge demanded.

"Your honor next up is docket number Q72351667 the people of New York versus Peter Baptiste." The DA was a late twenty-something year old well dressed white woman. She had an evil aura and for all of her nice clothes and makeup, she radiated viciousness. The moment Duane heard the prosecutor say 'the people of New York' it started to sink in how serious the charges against him were. Up until that time he was just a kid from South Side with a gun. He never imagined that all the people of New York would be trying him.

"Very well counselor. State your case against the defendant." The judge stated in a business like tone after the docket number was read.

"Your honor on Thursday, August twenty fifth of this year, the defendant Mr. Baptiste was sighted in South Jamaica beating and kicking another youth by two detectives from the one thirty first precinct. The young man who was being beaten refused to press charges. During the process of searching the defendant as he was being arrested on the scene, Detective Hinds and Detective Pazolli of the one-three-one, found a loaded and cocked nine millimeter Beretta. The defendant is currently on probation for another violent act and robbery charge that occurred only last year in Kings County. Due to the nature of his crime and violence in his juvenile record, the people move to have the defendant remanded to Rikers Island on a forthwith basis until a date for trail can be set. The people further request that that all requests for bail are denied on the grounds that the defendant has repeatedly exhibited a propensity for violence and is on the path to becoming a predicate felon." The D.A.'s voice was steely. She was out for a win and this seemed like an easy one. She would ask for the max on this one.

Though Duane was drenched in silent fear, his lawyer beside him looked like he was swatting flies. He stood up before the lady from the D.A.'s office could even sit down.

"Your honor Ira Silverman, of Silverman and associates…New York State number 113730." Duane's lawyer stated his license number to practice law in the state of New York as to let the stenographer enter him into the records.

"Your honor the peoples' request to hold bail is dramatic and excessive to say the least. Furthermore, he can't be judged because the people fear and hypothesize that he may become a predicate felon- he's to be judged solely on the facts of this case. My client is just a young man who lives in a rough neighborhood and has gotten mixed up in the wrong crowd. He's an honor roll student who comes from a good family with structure to it. I request that bail be set at a reasonable amount." Mr. Silverman countered.

"I agree to bail, counselor…bail is to be set at sixty thousand dollars." The judge stated.

"Sidebar your honor?" Mr. Silverman requested in a cynical tone.

"Counselor you and Ms. Wicowski may approach the bench." The judge said.

Silverman approached the bench, and in whispered tones addressed the judge. "Hey, how you doing, Ernie? Long time no see. Listen, I know the kid and his family, both his mother and aunt used to work for me. They run their own business out here in Queens and I know they don't have that type of money on hand. Their good people, Ernie and the boy is no hard rock. He's a misdirected, screwed up kid but locking him up like this is killing the family. Could you do me a personal favor and bring the bail down a couple of notches? Huh… would it kill you to do this one little thing for me, pal?" Mr. Silverman had known the judge on the professional and personal level for over twenty years.

"I don't have a problem with it…" The judge said slowly. "How about you Joan? What do you think?" The judge asked counselor Wicowski from the Queens County D.A. He had to give her some say in it or there'd be no living it down.

"Well…I don't want it to be less than a penny short than forty thousand. I want to make it as hard as possible for this kid to jump his bail." The prosecutor said.

The defense lawyer let out a loud exhale. "Is that a deal Ira?" The judge asked Mr. Silverman.

"Fair is fair…at least we can get bail." Mr. Silverman stated

The judge nodded. "O.K. but remember Ira you owe me one. I need to see you and Tanya at my event next week…you hear me?"

Silverman just winked his eye at the judge and smiled as he walked back to the defense table. The judge slammed his gavel and announced that bail was to be set at forty thousand dollars before he requested the next case on the calendar. Mr. Silverman saw the look both of Duane's parents had on their faces when the judge announced the amount of the bail. He pulled them to the side and told them not to worry because they only had to post ten percent of the bail to a bondsman in order to spring Duane from jail.

Mr. Silverman told them that he had a bail bondsman across from the court house on Queens Boulevard who would help them get Duane out when they came with ten percent of the bail. Hearing that they would only have to pay ten percent of the total bail was a great relief to Duane's family. Between their savings account and some petty cash that they had in the safe of the restaurant they were able to come up with the sudden eight thousand dollars that they had to spend. Four thousand went to place Mr. Silverman on a retainer, and the other four thousand of course went to the bail bondsman.

Duane had to sit tight in central booking a tad bit longer until his family could get all the money straight that day. Once they got the money to the bondsman and had him sprung, they brought him home and Jean began to whale on his son from the time he walked through the threshold. Jean beat Duane like he was a stranger in the street who stole something. Punching Duane all about his body and slapping him about the face before finally violently slamming him to the living room floor knocking the wind out of Duane. Duane who was still sore from the beating the police had put on him just lay there on the floor with a bewildered look on his face with his father standing over him looking deranged.

He never saw this violent side of his father before and was only saved by Winsome pulling Jean off of him while she begged him for mercy. As she held Jean back, she ordered Duane to get up and go take a shower before going straight to his room. As Duane slowly made his way across the living room toward the stairs, Winsome shadowed him blocking Jean from hitting him anymore. As he started to make his way up the stairs he whimpered the only response he could to the turmoil he'd caused his family.

"I'm sorry!" Duane stated.

"You're sorry...you're sorry...motherfucker you sure are sorry! I carry you for nine months...move fi America to make a better life for we. Mi work and go to school only fi have you embarrass this whole bumba clot family and go to jail? You sure are sorry!"

Winsome who rarely if ever at all used profanity slapped Duane so hard that spit flew from the corner of his mouth, leaving the impression of her right hand across his face.

CHAPTER NINE

Three months later, Duane went to trial and was found guilty of criminal possession of a weapon in the first degree. The prosecutor wanted to charge him as an adult and sentence him to three to five years in a medium security prison. That was their idea of being lenient. However, Mr. Silverman somehow persuaded the judge to charge Duane as a juvenile and sentence him to a year on Rikers Island in c-73. That was the best deal that he could be afforded and Mr. Silverman warned him that he was extremely lucky to have gotten any breaks with him being on probation already.

The bailiff escorted Duane from where he was seated with his lawyer through a door by the left side of the judge's bench of court room k-20 into a holding cell. He waited there until they had enough inmates to fill up the bus that was headed for Rikers Island. It seemed as if it took forever for the bus to come and Duane was in a real hurry to get his bid over with. Once they were on the white, orange and blue bus, the correctional officers who were transporting them cuffed the inmates to their seats and to each other two at a time just like Noah and the ark. Only this time there was only going to be men where they were going.

They finally left Queens central booking and were on their way down the Grand Central Parkway in route to "The Rock" as inmates called it. Once they got to the bridge Duane saw a sign that read "Welcome to Riker's Island Home of New York's Boldest". Then they crossed the bridge that connected the rest of Queens to Rikers Island which had to be at least a mile long before you even reached the actual facility. Duane and most of the inmates that were on the bus with him were let out and brought to a small filthy chain of holding cells which were used for intake.

There were men lying on the floor. There were others lucky and tough enough to lie across one of the three benches that were in the cell making everyone else have to stand. After about eight hours, they were moved from intake to the young men's building and given stiff tan prison jumpsuits, sheets, blankets and pillow cases for their bunks. The whole thing was a long drawn out hassle. After a few days of being in c-73, Duane came across his Brooklyn crew from when he was locked up in Spotford. Tony, Ka, and Khem explained that they caught a case together and had to do a year city time and had already been down for a month.

Once they all linked back up on Rikers, other crews didn't think about testing Duane. Before he came there, his crew had already been terrorizing the weaklings in their dorm and the rest of the facility. Several months went by and Duane's parents would pay him a visit at least every other week. Crossing that ominous bridge, going through all the metal detectors and being searched several times for a visit made them feel as though they were the ones who were actually in jail. Even though they dreaded going to the island they were his family so they put money in Duane's commissary account and visited when they could.

After seven and a half months of visiting Duane, they had become used to the hassle the guards would give them. On their last visit only two and a half weeks before they were scheduled to pick Duane up after his release, Jean and Winsome got into a heated argument as they made their way down the Grand Central Parkway. A large eighteen wheeler kept closely tailgating Jean as he drove. Jean tried switching lanes and continued the argument he and his wife were having about what they were going to do with Duane once he came home. The large rig still seemed to be following them, as if the driver was playing chicken with them. Jean switched lanes again and resumed making his point in the argument that he and Winsome were having.

All of a sudden, Jean felt the truck nudging him from behind. Once again he tried to move but it was too late. The front bumper had hooked itself to the back of the car somehow. The rig ran their car through a guard rail and into a tree, crushing it on impact. There was twisted metal, gas and shattered glass everywhere.

A few good Samaritans who witnessed the carnage made a futile attempt to get out of their vehicles and help pull Jean and Winsome out of the wreckage but their car was on fire and they believed the effort would be futile as there was no way they could have survived that crash. The car was demolished. All they could do without being burned themselves was to call for help from those little yellow phones on the side of the road. Fortunately, it was a short time before emergency service vehicles swarmed the area and the fire department used the Jaws of Life to pull them from the wreckage.

A week passed before Jean awoke from a coma in Jamaica hospital. He was burned over sixty percent of his body and was laid up in traction with the majority of the bones in his body broken or dislocated. When he came to Paul was there with P.J. and Raina. Paul shed tears of joy when he saw his father regain consciousness. He tried desperately to talk from under the oxygen mask he was wearing but Paul insisted that he get enough rest and save his strength. Jean wouldn't listen. He kept mouthing something but Paul couldn't hear what he was saying. He bent over closer to hear his father clearly. With all the strength Jean could muster, he strained as if he were yelling to ask a one word question. "Winsome?"

Paul twisted his face and took a deep breath, then began to sob uncontrollably. He shed a river of tears from his eyes. He was so heartbroken he couldn't even tell his father the tragic news at first. Then finally he let it all out in between sobbing in a sigh.

"She's…she's gone…mommy is gone. She died that day, dad."

Jean lay there in total and complete shock, as the emotional pain flooded his body. He couldn't believe it. It couldn't be true…things happened so fast and the last thing he could remember is her being by his side. He couldn't move a muscle laying there in traction beaten to a pulp, physically and spiritually. He was literally a broken man. All he could do was cry without blinking. The tears just flowed freely down his face as Paul hugged him and wiped them away. Jean was so heartbroken and disappointed to learn that the love of his entire life and best friend was gone forever! What bothered him most was that the last memory he had of her was the two of them arguing. After he laid there crying, some time into the night, Jean dozed off into an eternal sleep never to awaken again.

The doctors at the hospital said he'd died of internal bleeding that couldn't be stopped. However, his family knew better than that; Jean died of a broken heart. They knew that he'd lost the enchanted love of his life time and that was just a cross too heavy to bear. Every member of the family knew that's exactly what happened but Gwen was the only one to come out and say what they were all thinking about her brother- in-law's death.

The whole family, Gwen, Paul, along with China and P.J. went to Rikers the day after Jean's death and delivered the news to Duane. When he heard the news, he just absorbed his grief and stored it away in his throat. He wouldn't cry because in jail any sign of weakness or sharing your business with the wrong people could easily get you extremely hurt or even killed. He just nodded his head as they told him that under the circumstances he still had a week to be released but the Department of Corrections would let him out the next day to attend his parent's services.

That last night in jail, as he lay in his bunk, he was being eaten alive with guilt. He thought that when his parents didn't arrive for their final visit before he was to be released that they were just being cruel. He thought they were just striving to teach him some sort of lesson although he didn't know what that lesson could possibly be. Never in a million years could he fathom that something could actually be wrong with his parents. In his young mind, he thought that his parents would be around forever.

No, he'd never thought that both his parents would have to have the closed casket services they had. He never could have imagined the fire that had broken out in the car would have burned Winsome beyond any possible recognition the way that it did. He never could have imagined Jean being almost ripped in two by the car's engine on impact with that tree. Never could he fathom his father having a closed casket because the look of sorrow he had on his face when he leaned that his precious Winsome was gone. His face couldn't be fixed into another fashion by the mortician. He never would have thought that he'd have to cremate his parents' earthly remains at the end of his city bid and leave them at the mausoleum on Francis Lewis Boulevard.

After he attended their services at Gillmont funeral home on Linden Boulevard he thought that this all was just a bad dream he'd wake up from shortly. Yet and still reality started to sink in once he got home and started to take off his dress clothing. He prepared to celebrate their memory in the traditional nine night celebration. He did his best to ease his pain after the nine night celebration was over by hanging out with his crew and Keisha. He also kept company with several other females who he was seeing before he went away.

Coming home was bitter sweet because his crew threw him a party and he was free. No more having to fight with the rest of those wild adolescents in the dorm. No more late night M.O. watch (Mental Observation) and no more correctional officers waking him up at five in the morning. No more correctional officers then screaming five minutes later "walkin' out for chow!" He was happy to be back in the streets that raised him where he belonged. No more of that stale prison air at 1010 Hazen Street on Rikers Island, East Elmhurst New York. Yes sir, he was back in good old South Jamaica but now with both his parents gone it felt like a piece of him was missing.

About a month or so after he got home, he found out that that he was going to be an uncle. Paul and Raina were going to have a child in approximately seven months or so. At first they didn't want to say anything because Raina wasn't completely sure she was pregnant. Duane was delighted to hear the news because even though he lost his parents, he'd be gaining a nephew or a niece.

Paul and Duane were sixteen now and Gwen was awarded legal guardianship of the twins after both their parents met their demise. They guy who was driving the truck that killed Jean and Winsome worked for a large Arab oil company called Beneficent. It was found that the driver was drunk and high on cocaine the day he ran Jean and winsome off the road. Despite his being visibly impaired at the depot, the foreman had made the decision to send him out anyway rather than have to rearrange the delivery. He was later found guilty of criminally negligent homicide and charged with two counts of murder for both of their deaths. Beneficent was a new company in the states and they didn't want any negative press so they did what any of their American counterparts would have done…settle out of court.

Gwen had an attorney from Mr. Silverman's firm represent her interest in the matter. After the smoke cleared and all was said and done Beneficent settled on a seven million dollar wrongful death agreement which was paid to the family. Three point five million was paid for Jean and three point five million was paid for Winsome. Gwen was the twin's legal guardian until they turned eighteen so she automatically had the power of attorney over her sister's estate since Winsome didn't have a will. When it was all said and done Gwen and the boys were left with roughly five million after the lawyer fees were deducted.

Two point five million was put away in a secured account under the twins name that neither one of them would be allowed to touch until they turned twenty one. Gwen decided that she would use the other half of the money to take care of the boys with. There was also a two hundred fifty thousand dollar life insurance policy that Jean and Winsome had been paying into for years. She finished paying the remaining balances of both mortgages of Winsome's home as well as her own. She also decided to expand the restaurant by adding a patio where her customers could sit outside and eat if they chose to. She also rented out the patio for large catered events and other various functions.

Gwen still lived in South Jamaica but she'd secretly purchased a condo in the upper class Forest Hills neighborhood of Queens for her and her boyfriend Gordon. Being as though she had to tend to the restaurant and her man so much she couldn't always come through and check on her nephews as much as she should have or wanted to. She'd only make it there to the house on 178th street in person about two or three times a week for about an hour or so every time she'd visit. Other than that she'd just call the twins here and there. Besides they were practically grown men in her eyes and as Paul had a child on the way, what could she possibly tell them?

By this time P.J. had repeatedly fallen out with Gwen's young lover and ended up moving to the Castle in Flatbush where China was still the super. After the horrific deaths of both Jean and Winsome, China fell into a deep depression and began drinking heavily. He was only sober half the time now and that was the time when he'd have to alert the owner of the building to a problem or the people from the rental office were around.

P.J. was now a freshman at Erasmus Hall, the local high school on Flatbush Ave. and ran with a wild bunch of kids who were into boosting clothes. In an attempt to emulate Duane's go getter criminal state of mind, P.J. would steal thousands of dollars of Polo clothing and sell it for half price. Hell at this point China was so drunk half the time that he didn't even bother to ask where his son got the clothes or money from.

Paul had moved Raina in with him so he could keep a closer eye and her and their child that was growing inside of her. Gwen gave the boys some of their money and let Paul buy himself a brand new Acura Legend. Duane took his portion of the monies Gwen was rationing out and brought four bricks of the rawest cocaine he could get his hands on with it. He figured he could whip himself up a brand new German automobile, flashy jewels and an arsenal of big guns with that in no time flat.

All he had to do was mix the coke he purchased in with the rest of the product he and Shiz were selling for The Family anyway. He bought the yayo from Donnell and told him that they were gradually going to be raising money so he and Shiz could buy weight wholesale and they would keep the spot on Sutton Boulevard as their own, if it was all right with him. It was more than all right with Donnell. As his underlings elevated in stature, so did he and not only would he have less of a headache worrying if those guys were going to bring back all the money they were supposed to on time but he'd get a bigger kickback now that they were copping wholesale. Deep down, Donnell was proud of his little prodigy for thinking big and wielding his cunning organizational skills to expand his brand and boss up.

Things had changed dramatically since Duane had been locked up this time around. There was so much money being made in the drug trade at this time people were becoming rich just by selling hand to hand. Just by working in the building of their complex, Junior and Terry now were both driving brand new 318 and 325 drop top B.M.W's respectively. Shiz had advanced to a brand spanking new black on black Mercedes Benz 300e with a spoiler kit and ground effects. Donnell also stepped up his automobile game. He was now driving a smoke grey S.500 Mercedes Benz or a Big Boy as the locals referred to it in the neighborhood.

Duane played it cool at first when he got home. He laid low and decided to just observe who was doing what before he made a move. He wasn't about to be outdone by any of his crew especially when he used to consider them under his wing. He just kept on buying product from Donnell and organized another retail location around the corner from their original spot that was in the vicinity of Sutton Boulevard. He wanted the nice cars and neighborhood fame but valued creating longevity for his new operation more than having the quick flash like everyone else did.

His mind had become very strategic during his last bid. In between playing razor tag and fighting with other inmates Duane found time to read Sun Tzu's ancient text The Art of War. The way he looked at it he was at war with all the big time people with a name in the drug game in New York City who were truly getting paid. To live and die by the rules of the N.Y. hustle game was his motto. He decided to bring in his crew of hooligans from Brooklyn even though he still had Donnell's goons behind him since he was down with The Family.

He wanted the recognition and respect that came from being with The Family. However, he also wanted to be his own man and that meant being able to create his own identity as a leader, separate from The Family. He brought in Tony, Ka, and Ka's younger brother Khem as muscle, which was a strategic move on his part. He did it to instill fear in the locals who weren't apart of his inner circle. He didn't want to be in a position where longtime loyalties and friendship would make him diplomatic instead of being ruthless with people who fucked up.

Because these cats from Brownsville and East New York didn't know any of his peoples from Queens, they wouldn't have a problem in the slightest with tearing anyone of them apart if Duane said so. Duane was trying to move smarter now that he'd done some time for beating down one of his workers. He knew for sure his Brooklyn massive would handle themselves well in a tight situation if one were ever to arise so justice would still be meted out. Plus he was a boss now and he couldn't always personally get his hands dirty...that's what the guys from Brownsville and East New York were for.

One day while he was on Linden Boulevard with Sherman and Ka, Duane happened to bump into Gwen's boyfriend Gordon. Gordon scoped him up and down and noticed that Duane was dipped in well over three thousand dollars worth of Gucci and tens of thousands of dollars worth of truck jewelry. Gordon was a local guy like Duane and his family and was also of Jamaican decent as well.

Duane never had an occasion or reason to ask Gordon exactly what he did for his living. He just knew that Gordon took damn good care of his aunt every since they started dating. Gordon wasn't a slouch either...he was live in his own little way too. He was a brown shinned chap about ten years younger than Gwen and stood approximately five foot eight with a receding hairline and wore a lot of heavy dark colored gold from the Caribbean.

Gordon approached Duane and pulled him to the side to converse with him for a moment. They chatted for about five minutes and went their separate ways after Duane jotted down his number. Gordon told Duane that he heard how large Duane was making a point to put it out there that he had top of the line product at wholesale rates whenever Duane was ready to do business. Duane's ego was a little stroked by having this older cat approach him on a business call. The word was out about Duane and his crew now…they were really gettin' money and he knew he was becoming a major player by the way the streets were talking about him.

After only a few months of being home everything was going fine for Duane. He decided to move Kiesha into the house along with him, his brother, and Raina. At first everything was just fine in the house until a few months later Raina and Kiesha began acting catty around one another. Initially, Duane and Paul had things under control until one day when neither of their men was around. Kiesha and Raina got into a heated altercation over Raina catching Kiesha doing a few lines of coke in the bathroom. Raina started to raise her voice and told Kiesha that she didn't want any drugs in the house, especially since she was pregnant.

"Aww hell no...I know I ain't even just catch you all up in my house takin' a motha fuckin' bump! Check this out here...I'm about to have a child and we don't need that shit in this house. You understand me, missy? Don't let me catch you pingin' that junk in here again or it's gonna be some real serious problems up in this bitch...you hear me?" Raina yelled with her hand on her hip, in the bathroom's doorway.

"See...that's where you're wrong." Kiesha shot back. "This ain't even none of your business. This house belongs to my man and his brother. So don't even try to pull rank on me, missy. As far as a problem... it could be whatever, bitch!" Kiesha rose to full attention from where she was bent over the sink holding a small mirror and a straw, defiantly wiping the caked up excess powder from her nostrils.

"If I wasn't four months pregnant I would slap fire out of your little simple minded young ass! Don't worry, though I won't be pregnant for ever...watch, bitch... you just watch and see what happens in a minute!"

"That's what the fuck I thought, bitch!" Kiesha replied, with her hands on her hips rolling her eyes and bobbing her head rhythmically from side to side simultaneously with her every word that came out of her mouth, sucking her teeth disrespecting Raina.

Raina clocked Kiesha dead in the mouth, four months pregnant and all. The two began scuffling back and forth in the hall way knocking down portraits of Jean and Winsome off the wall in the process. Paul just happened to walk in down stairs and heard the commotion up stairs and ran to break up the ruckus. After a few minutes both Kiesha and Raina had calmed down enough to explain to Paul exactly what happened. Paul couldn't believe what he was hearing. To him, that was the straw that broke the camel's back. He instructed Raina to stay away from Kiesha until he could talk to his brother and sort everything out personally one on one.

A few hours later Duane arrived home and the fireworks officially began!

"A yo we got a problem, man! You and your girl need to find some other living arrangements like yesterday. While you were gone she was in here, violating our house... the same house mommy and daddy bust their asses so that we could have a decent place to live." Paul stated in an urgent rage.

Not sure of exactly what Paul was talking about, Duane just mumbled something under his breath then let it all come out at once. "Slow the fuck down...what the fuck is you talkin' about my man?"

"I'm talkin' bout your coke head old lady doing that junk in the mother fuckin' house, that's what nigga!" Paul stated as he confronted his brother with the news of Kiesha being caught in the act.

"First of all, she not no coke head...she just occasionally sniffs from time to time and it ain't no big ass deal like you making it out to be. Maybe you should take a ping too so you can stop being such a tight ass and take it down a thousand. Relax yourself and watch how the fuck you talk to me!" Duane shot back, agitated.

"Watch how I talk to you...homey I ain't one of your flunkies or any of those herbs you roll with out in the street. This is me...I'm your blood and I'm tellin' you that your girl gotta go. She put her hands on my lady while she's pregnant and you know that's total and complete violation." Paul demanded.

"Relax man...I got this! Let me talk to her and see what happened. You know how females are. Just cool out and be easy!" Duane reasoned

"Nah you not hearing me the broad has to go" Said Paul.

"Who the fuck is you callin' a broad, B…I know you ain't trying to diss my girl! I hope you don't think that baby is really yours either. I heard that she's a stunt in the projects and that baby could be for anybody. She got your lame ass fooled…right? What she wanted a sucker to put that little bastard child on? You know how it go momma's baby and daddy's maybe. So don't you ever in your long legged life try and disrespect my lady." Duane said getting more and more animated with every breath he took at that point.

"You heard me!" Paul would not back down.

"Oh word? I know you don't want no beef for real-for real, you little basketball playin' Michael Jordan wanna be sucka ass nigga! Boy I'll fly your head if you ever try and raise your bitch ass hands to me!" Duane was in his gorilla stance, enraged at his brother's defiance.

"See that's your problem. You think it's all about you but it's not! The baby Raina is having is your blood asshole, but you're too busy playing cops and robbers to think about that shit though, ain't you?" Paul shook his head in disgust, not knowing how to reason with a brother that was so far gone. He didn't know Duane anymore, he realized.

"See, that's what the fuck I'm talkin' about! I got enough static with real killers and the police to be worrying about your square ass and be going through all this sucka shit when I come home. That's my mother fuckin' word to mommy and daddy nigga, if you wasn't my blood I'd drag my steel on your chump ass for tryin' to bass me like that! Just get the fuck out of my face and I'll pretend like I didn't hear you and none of this ever even happened!" Duane said attempting to shut Paul down.

Normally it would have been over with that being said. Paul knew that Duane packed guns and heard of several people coming up missing because of it. But these were not a normal set of circumstances and they weren't little kids anymore. The stakes were very high and Paul knew that he was in the right.

"Nah nigga this shit ain't over. You gonna listen to what the fuck I got to say! See it's one thing for you to be slingin' that shit out in the streets but don't be bringing that shit around me and my family. Plus you the biggest asshole I know! You over there in the projects all these years trying to be a hardrock and shit while Mommy and Daddy bust their asses so we could come to this country and make it. They gave us everything... you ain't never want for nothing...not one single solitary thing. Yet you out there selling crack, trying to get a little name for yourself!" He took a deep breath, all the pent up anger boiling to the top.

"Just how fuckin' stupid could you be? See the difference between you and them dudes from the 'jects is that they do that shit so they can eat and have clothes on their back. Here it is, you're a millionaire right now and you cold playin' yourself out living your phony little Al Pachino fantasies. You ain't no real gangster, you wanna know who was a real gangster…daddy that's who! Daddy was a mother fuckin' gangster! He went to work every day and took being called a fuckin' coconut and a banana boat so we could have food on our table. He took whatever job he had to take to feed us too."

"Plus you don't even know why we're here in America do you? Daddy caught like nine or ten bodies in Jamaica because some faggot nigga named Dexter was tryin' to play him and disrespect mommy. Bet your dumb ass didn't know that, did you? Why you think we never been down there, dummy? Nah you never knew about any of that 'cause daddy told me, not your stupid ass because he knew you would have tried to play the gangster role.

Well guess what? You a fuckin' punk…and my father was a gangster because he took care of all of his family no matter what. That's a gangster!" Paul stated with vigor as he finished his longwinded diatribe.

"But…but" Duane attempted to make a rebuttal, however nothing would come out of his mouth except for the word 'but'.

"Shut the fuck up and don't even try to say another word, nigga! I was the one that had to go to the morgue and see mommy's skin burned the fuck up like that! She was burned so bad the only way I knew it was her for sure was because of the ring daddy gave her. I was the one who had to tell daddy she was dead when he was laid up in the hospital all broke the fuck up like that. I was the one that had to watch him die after he cried like a baby when I told him mommy was gone. Nigga, you ain't never seen our father cry about a damn thing in his entire mother fuckin' life!"

"I was there not you…where were you? Oh I forgot. Locked up 'cause you wanna be runnin' behind Sherman and them perpetrating a fraud like you Tony Montana…fuck outta here! You killed them! You killed them…you killed them, you punk motherfucker! If they weren't going to Riker's Island to see you, they'd still be alive. You killed them… you killed them for real with all your fake shit." Paul stated in a manner that was uncharacteristic of his normal pedigree. In his anger he shed tears of resentment and frustration that burned his face as if they were acid.

His words burned Duane to the core because he did feel guilty for his parent's demise as well. With the tension being so thick and without anything else he could say without the two brothers literally killing one another Duane decided to leave. He gathered a few belongings from upstairs in his bedroom including a portrait of his parents and left with Kiesha in tow. The very next day, he sought Sincere out and enlisted his aid in getting an apartment. Sincere agreed but could see something was amiss with Duane. Sincere who had become a father figure to Duane in Jean's absence asked his surrogate son what was wrong. Duane told him everything that happened between him and Paul except for the part about the money.

"I'm not taking any one's side but the side of the truth and your brother is a little right on this one, D. He's right about letting your dirt effect the people around you. You're your own man and are gonna do what you're gonna do. Just give the people around you a chance to choose for themselves if they're gonna allow themselves to be effected by your dirt or not. You have to at least give them a fair chance to have their own free will in the matter." Sincere stated giving his take on what he'd just heard.

"I'm speaking from experience…see I never told you all the details of why I got locked up before. I always speak about getting caught for that armed robbery… which was stupid enough by itself but I never told you exactly how I got caught. See, I was with my little cousin that day who was his mother's only son. I told him to go in to the bank with me but I didn't tell him I was about to rob the joint."

"I pulled the job off with him standing there looking shocked that I just hopped over the counter with that big ass four fifth long and was about to get away carrying a bag with over one hundred thousand stashed away in it. Since I didn't tell him what we were going into the bank for he just froze on the spot. As I was trying to pull at him to come on so we could get away one of the armed guards took five shots at me and missed, hitting him all five times in his back as well as his head."

"He got hit up and I still could have got away, but I didn't want to leave my family lying there dying like that with no one by his side. That's exactly how I got caught because I hesitated! I should have never involved him in that shit and he still would have been alive till this day. At the very least I should have told him what I was going to do and I'd have a much cleaner conscience right now."

"Look, I know you're out here and you're doing your thing! I didn't want to say anything before but your little name is starting to ring some major bells right now. That's cool if that's the life you choose, like I said you're your own man. I'd like you to do something else with your life because you are very talented as well as intelligent and as I said before intelligence controls all things! However, I'm not going to force you to do anything because you have your own free will."

"See, as far as I'm concerned you're a man now…a very young man but nevertheless, a man. It's going to be you that has to pay the price if you keep getting caught up by the law. See, you think shit is sweet because so far you only been doing those little juvy skid bids in adolescent facilities here and there. Well, I got some news for you…you're a big boy now. Just look at your crew, cats seventeen and eighteen pushin' drop-top Beemers and Benz's. Don't be fooled and think that the man ain't watching you, young God, because he is!"

"For whatever reason I see you call yourself playing it low key in that little Jetta of yours, which is cool. But just remember that I told you the next time they catch you, you're not just gonna have to go to the island. They're gonna ship your ass up north to adult medium and maximum security facilities or maybe even the feds. I don't know all of your business and I don't want to know but the streets are talking and they are saying as far as all the young hustlers that you're the real deal."

"Like I said you can do what you want to do, because it's your life…my job is to make knowledge born by warning you about the road you're headed down. I'm not gonna stand here and beat you in the head all day either, just remember what I said and don't get your family involved with your dirt if that's not what they choose to do. Just by being as large as you are in the cipher you deal in and you living with them, it was eventually gonna cause a problem."

"Plus, y'all shouldn't have had two young girls living under the same roof anyway…y'all was asking for a headache with that one! Women are like planets in the solar system and you have to give them their proper space to rotate around their sun…which would be you, her man. If two planets enter each other's orbit then the results could be catastrophic, as you can see. A woman can be your heaven or your hell. It's strictly up to you to choose which one you want her to be though."

"Long story short, just let your brother be man. He has a very good chance of actually going to college and making something of himself…so just let him be for the time being. Don't think that I'm getting you this apartment because of the money you're paying me either. I'm doing it strictly because you're my little man. And so your activities in the street won't fuck up your brother's prospects of becoming college material. As far as the money, I'm going to use that to get some equipment for the other boys I mentor with it.

If you're not careful, word is bond I guarantee you that you'll find yourself surrounded by three things death, hell, and destruction! This I promise you, but like I said, it's your choice."

Duane liked talking to Sincere in general but especially about life. Usually things were clearer immediately after he spoke to the older man but this conversation had a much more serious tone to it as Sincere analyzed what was happening between him and his brother.

CHAPTER TEN

Sincere and Duane looked for a suitable apartment for a few days then finally decided on a spacious two bedroom with hard cherry wood floors. It was in an exclusive secluded building with a doorman a few blocks north of Hillside Avenue in the Briarwood section of Queens not far from the Van Wyck expressway. That suited Duane just fine because he was still in Queens but far enough away from where he did his business that people couldn't watch his every movement. Yet he was still close enough to be wherever he had to be in almost a blink of an eye.

Sincere got Duane the apartment by saying he would be moving in with his nephew. Also by tipping the lady at the rental office five thousand extra dollars Duane had given him to make sure there wouldn't be any problems moving in. Just two weeks later, Duane and Paul's seventeenth birthday arrived. This was the moment Duane had been waiting for - all the while he was saving money and buying all those kilos of cocaine from Donnell and The Family led up to his birthday.

Duane treated himself to a brand new gold on black drop top Saab nine hundred with B.B.S. rims on it. In addition he also bought a dark navy blue B.M.W. 733I with custom made cream interior also with B.B.S. rims for his birthday. He kept his Jetta and left it plain so he could use it for transporting illicit materials as well as a down low everyday car. From time to time, he would let Kiesha drive it when he didn't need to use it for anything.

By the time Duane started flashing a little bit of his earnings, he was the talk of the whole neighborhood because no one except for his inner circle really knew how much money he was really making. They still truly didn't even know either because Duane never actually let others on to his true worth. They lusted for the flash and the immediate self gratification the game brought them. However, Donnell saw how long of a run The Family was having with little to no interruption by the authorities. Both Duane and Donnell saw that control and organization would be the key to longevity in their chosen career paths.

Everything was going exactly how Duane had planned it. He built his money up and began purchasing his own product and an arsenal of heavy weapons for his crew. He made sure that everyone in his faction was more than fairly compensated for whatever work that they were putting in so things would run smoothly. Then the unthinkable happened...Germ and Link were picked up by the feds on a conspiracy beef.

The government said that they had a star witness against them that could confirm they were running a continuing criminal enterprise. They separated the two brothers, housing Link in Fort Dix New Jersey, and Germ in Farrington N.J. two federal facilities within the tri-state federal jail circuit. They didn't want to place them in any facility in the state of New York for fear that they could bribe guards or somehow still call shots from their jail cells. In some cases, that would allow security to be compromised if they could influence other inmates or even Federal corrections officers with their money and clout. Ironically, their father was scheduled to be coming home in a year's time of their arrest.

After Duane had finished knocking off the three kilos of coke that he last got from Donnell before Link and Jerm got tied up by the feds, things dried up for their operation faster than the speed of light. Without The Family supplying them with product, things went from sugar to shit in no time. Desperate for product, Duane tried to deal with a few connects he had uptown but the quality they had for the price wasn't balancing out the hassle for him. And he didn't like the risk of going all the way uptown to transport large quantities of drugs from an area that was well known for drug trafficking. It just wasn't worth the risk to him.

Then one day while checking in on Gwen at the restaurant her boyfriend Gordon happened to be there as well as Dorrine and Paul. Duane had totally forgotten about the proposition Gordon gave him a few months earlier in regards to supplying him with some product. After he was finished talking to his aunt and cousin, he pulled Gordon to the side in the front of the restaurant to have a little talk with him. All while passing his brother by and not saying one peep to him. The two spoke and Gordon let it be known that he had a Cuban connection out in Havana that he could get as much coke as Duane wanted or needed whenever he was ready. He didn't really want to deal with Gordon but he agreed to out of sheer desperation. They set a deal up for five kilos the next day in the afternoon.

The next day came and as agreed, Duane purchased five kilos of product from Gordon at $14,500.00 a piece. Duane really and truly wanted more but went light for what he really wanted on the first trip out with Gordon. Things went smoother than Duane could have ever imagined or expected. By there suddenly being a drought in the neighborhood, the fiends were thirsty to get their fixes.

There also were some wholesale customers who were in need of some ounces as well. In two days flat Duane had completely finished serving up the five thousand grams of raw he got from Gordon. Duane was very pleased at the response that he got from his customers this time around as well. They said that it was just as good if not better than what they got served though Donnell and The Family.

Duane decided to turn it all the way up and take things to a higher level. The next time he made an order with Gordon it was for twenty kilos...a whole seven hundred and twenty ounces. Which was twenty thousand one hundred and sixty grams of pure profit as far as Duane was concerned. To make every ki last even longer he decided to add a small amount of lactose to them to stretch his profit margin even farther. This was the most product that Duane had ever dealt with in his young life.

He called a meeting with Donnell and told him that he had all the product needed to fill the void that Link and Germ left and they could be partners. He proposed to supply Donnell with all of the cocaine he would need to run the buildings on both sides of New York Boulevard as he'd done previously under Link and Germ. In turn, Duane would receive a much larger cut for his efforts since he would now in effect be a General instead of just a lieutenant. In short Duane was now a young boss who was calling major shots and gradually taking over a large portion of the drug trade in his area.

He made Sherman the lieutenant who would oversee his whole operation. Terry had become good at mixing and cutting different product so they made him head of mixing, stretching and cooking all the cocaine that would be transformed into crack. Junior and Terry would also serve as eyes and ears of the projects keeping workers in line when Donnell was away and would report directly to Sherman. At first there were a few glitches with some people getting used to Duane being the new boss in the projects.

However after a few visits from Ka and Tony and a few guys being ruthlessly pistol whipped and others who were in violation coming up shot in the head, things bounced back into ship shape. Now that Duane had the product, muscle, and organization part of being a boss down there was a major part of being in charge he didn't know about... paying off Johnny law. Donnell schooled him to that aspect of the game and told him the pay roll for the crooked cops they had in pocket would be fifty thousand a month. A small price to pay for an organization that grossed approximately a little over one point five million dollars a month between the projects and the spots they had on Sutton Boulevard.

Duane was very skeptical about giving those cops that type of money at first because in his mind he thought if that was the case why didn't they warn Link and Germ about the indictment that was coming down on them. Duane explained that they caught a federal case and that there was a rat involved in their case. However as far as the local guys, Donnell was familiar with an officer and his partner. They recently transferred from the 131st precinct to the high intensity drug unit of the Queens Task Force South. He said that he'd done business with them for years and that's how their operation managed to stay afloat before for so long with little to no problems.

Donnell insisted that it was essential to their business to pay these police off, especially since they had transferred to that new unit. They would be able to give them a heads up about when the raids were going to be and which building they were going to be hitting. In addition to information about anybody in their crew or anyone else for that matter who were cooperating with the authorities against their operation. It took a little persuasion but eventually Duane trusted Donnell's judgment and went along with the plan. They were to meet both the two detectives on Broad Channel Drive out in the Far Rockaway section of Queens in a diner.

Later on that day when they met the detectives Duane couldn't believe who it was. Detectives Hinds and Pazolli…the same two cops who had busted him on his first gun charge! Duane immediately felt uncomfortable understandably but once they sat down and spoke they let him know that they never would have busted his balls if they knew he was down with The Family. As they sat there in the greasy spoon of a diner they gave Donnell and Duane some very disturbing news…somebody in their crew was ratting.

They couldn't say who it was by name just yet because the paperwork they had in reference to the matter listed the snitch as a C.I. (confidential informant).

The detectives warned them to be very careful in all of their dealings and to watch every member their crew. They said that the task force knew exactly where they were keeping their stash in the Bedell Houses and for them to change the location of where they kept and mixed it as often as possible. They informed them to do so because in order for them to execute a successful raid they'd have to get a warrant for the specific location they were raiding. In the end, Duane was glad that he met those dirty cops and slid them that book bag stuffed with money. Now, there was no problem with giving them the money they were demanding every month because it was in trade, a small price for him to pay. He had to pay the cost to be the boss because to him staying free on the streets was priceless!

From then on, Duane told Donnell that they were going to start doing things a tad bit different. They were going to shut down their retail operations for a short while and go totally wholesale. This way it would eliminate who Duane thought was the rat. He had his suspicions but still didn't want to believe that it could actually be true. To stay afloat, they would wholesale to their wholesale clients and to a new client named Rock from Philly who was buying major weight.

Duane got connected to Rock through Niemah a bombshell of a young girl who all the young guys in the neighborhood nicknamed "Bedroom Eyes". She was related to Shadele, a girl who'd lived upstairs from his aunt and used to babysit Duane when he was younger and they'd lived on Fitch Boulevard. Niemah ended up moving down to Philly because of some of her father's street activity and she loved hustlers. She was dating Rock at the time and he needed a strong connect in New York and got plugged into Duane through her.

They decided to keep their flow the same in their spot on Sutton Boulevard and Donnell wholeheartedly agreed with Duane that it was a good idea to close shop in Bedell for a while. A few days later Duane went through Rosenberg Village in his new BMW to check on one of his lady friends whom he'd occasionally have liaisons with. Along the way, he came across Alex on Farmers Boulevard and 137th street. Alex who was driving a brand spanking new black Mercedes Benz 300E flagged Duane down. He wanted to talk for a minute.

They pulled over near the Long Island Rail Road train trestle. Duane almost had to choke down the rush of pride and excitement he felt when Alex told him that he wanted to do business with him. He said he heard through the grapevine that Duane was the man to see now that Link and Germ were in federal custody. Duane smiled a little smile but didn't say one word. He took his number and told him he'd contact him as soon as he had something. As soon as Alex hopped in his car and sped off Duane ripped his number into tiny little shreds and threw it in a storm drain. He was too paranoid after speaking with those cops and couldn't trust anybody that had any dealings with Link and Germ before they got busted.

Duane's plan was to deal directly with Rock from Philly which would be a solid come up for him being as Rock purchased no less than six kilos at a time. He was going full speed ahead with the plan to shut down the retail operation in the projects. Later on that very same day, after he came back from checking the female in Rosenberg, he had Kiesha drive him to Bedell so he could collect the last of the retail money from all the buildings and a few guns that Terry was holding for him. He collected the guns from Terry and put them in a small black leather Gucci bag which he stashed in the trunk of his car.

He instructed Kiesha to drive very carefully and do the speed limit all the way back to the apartment. As they made their way down Fitch toward Merrick Boulevard, Duane kept noticing what appeared to be an undercover police car on their tail. By the time they reached Merrick, Duane found out that sure enough, he was right. It was the police and they were pulling them over. Duane instructed Kiesha to say his name was Paul and that his car was for his aunt since it was bought in Gwen's name.

The cops who pulled them over were plainclothes detectives but said that they pulled them over because Kiesha didn't use her blinker when she turned onto Merrick Boulevard. Duane found that to be mighty peculiar for detectives but then he knew for sure that something was wrong when they demanded to search the car. They didn't find anything illegal in the car and Duane could tell that they were getting oh so pissed off by how crimson red their faces were turning. Then one of the detectives opened the glove compartment and pressed the button that opened the trunk. Once they searched the trunk they discovered the two black semi automatic forty fives in the Gucci bag under the spare tire in the trunk.

Duane ended up taking the rap for the guns and told them that his name was Paul because he knew his brother had a squeaky clean record. He knew that if they ran his real name that he'd end up under the jail for his second gun charge in less than three years. The police took them both to the station house and separately questioned Duane and Kiesha. Like a soldier, Kiesha ran the exact script he told her to.

The car wasn't in her name and Duane took the rap for guns. The police wanted to know what a seventeen year old was doing with ten thousand dollars in cash and guns in the trunk of a car that cost more than they made in two years. Duane hung his head when they asked him that because he knew that it was at least fifty thousand in the trunk and realized he had been fleeced by the cops that pulled him over.

"I'm not saying jack shit until my lawyer gets here, you flatfoot beat walkin' mother fuckers!" Duane stated defiantly. He had called Silverman as his legal representation.

Unfortunately for Duane, it wouldn't be till the next day that they took him to central booking. When he finally did get arraigned the next day they set his bail at thirty thousand dollars and gave him a trial date four months later from that exact day. He called Donnell who came and posted the ten percent of the full amount that they were asking for.

A few months went by and Gwen's health deteriorated rapidly. One day, she suddenly had to be hospitalized at Sloan Kenneling Hospital in Manhattan on First Ave and 67th street. All of the kids were the last to receive the tragic news. Gwen had cancer and was dying rapidly. She decided to go to Sloan because they are one of the best facilities to treat cancer in the world. That still wouldn't make a difference in the end though.

Gwen had actually started being treated for cancer about a year before Jean and Winsome were killed. She kept the suffering to herself and Gordon. She thought that the chemotherapy treatment that they were giving her was making her sicker than the actual cancer itself. She couldn't figure out the exact cause of her ailment either. But in theory, the doctors told her that she may have contracted the disease in her original basement apartment when she first moved to America. She didn't smoke so that was the only thing that they could come up with. They said that she had probably been contaminated by asbestos and the lead paint that they used in that old house.

One day Duane went to pay Gwen a visit to get all the matters with the money straight before she was to meet her demise. Sad to say yet her family had to come to terms with her dying because she simply didn't have any fight left in her anymore and they all could tell the end was at hand.

"Duane, I affi make a confession to you." Gwen said in a low weak voice trying her best to speak over the noisy respirator on the right hand side of her bed as Duane held her hand.

"Yes, Auntie speak, I'm listening." Duane said softly.

"I don't want you to think I'm horrible for what I've done, promise me when I tell you this that you won't think I'm horrible…you promise." Gwen said with her voice trailing off.

"Never Auntie…never in a million years." Duane said earnestly, holding her hand.

"Winsome was mi little sister and your father was my family too but I must tell you I spent all of the money that wasn't in the bank for you until you turn twenty one."

Gwen shamefully admitted.

"All of it Auntie?" He couldn't believe that "How'd you spend that much in less than two years…I don't understand!" Duane was trying not to blow his cool. He wanted to be understanding as his aunt lay on her death bed.

"Understand, I knew I was dying and I just wanted to have a little fun with Gordon... Plus mi buy you the cars dem and both the houses cause I know I didn't have long to live." Gwen stated coming completely clean.

"Yes I understand that...but what does Gordon have to do with the money being missing...do he have anything to do with you spending all of that money?"
Duane asked flatly.

"Just a little bit...the rest I spent." Gwen admitted.

"Take it easy aunt and just tell me the truth I promise I won't be mad if you tell me the truth...just tell me the truth, Auntie!" Duane stated in a desperate tone of voice.

"Well I was in so much pain all over my body...I just wanted and needed something to ease the blood clot pain. I am dying and was ready fi try anything to ease the pain. So Gordon give me some coke...he tell me say it would ease the pain. It does but it won't stop me from dying!" Gwen was sobbing now, the shame making it hard to keep her eyes from the floor.

"You spent all the money snorting coke?" Duane candidly asked as he stroked her hand softly.

"I spent a lot of it on snorting coke, but I also gave Gordon some money so he can get some coke fi sell it and make money. Please don't be mad at me...please don't be mad!" Gwen stated through gruff wheezes as Duane firmly held her hand.

"I told you auntie; never in a million years... never...don't you worry yourself. Get your rest so you can come home and run the restaurant you and mommy started, hear?" Duane said as Paul walked through the door with P.J.

"Another thing..." She said weakly. "The two of you need to stop fighting. Promise me that you will... promise me that ...just promise!"

Still holding his dying aunt by the hand, Duane just gave her a cold plastic smile and shook his head in a motion as if to say that he would honor her request yet never verbally acknowledged her. Things were getting a little bit too emotional for Duane's taste plus he had the disturbing news about Gordon and Gwen spending half the money to deal with. He thought back to what Sincere told him because he saw people in his life dying around him or destroying their lives going to jail for a very long time.

Truth be told, he also gave a little thought to the conversation he and his brother had a few months earlier. He was also thinking of how his plans of doubling the money Gwen was supposed to be holding for him were now ruined. He'd become accustomed to living the high life and he couldn't imagine life any other way. He'd learned that if properly used that money was a powerful weapon, and he wanted to be armed to the teeth with it.

He was cross with his aunt but there was no reason to punish her more than the disease ravaging her body already was. "Relax and get your rest Auntie. Mrs. Willcott is going to be needing you at the restaurant soon. I have to go now but I'll be back to visit with you tomorrow, ok?"

That was the last thing he said in his aunt's general direction. P.J. and Paul were now by her side. He walked slowly out the door backwards then he disappeared into the hallway. He made it to his car and took the upper roadway of the nearby Queens Bridge with the majestic Manhattan skyline behind him. Duane had lived in New York all of his life with the exception of a few months as an infant but still marveled at the architecture of the city especially when he would cross the Queens Bridge. From up there he could see the Williamsburg Bridge, the Manhattan Bridge, and the world famous Brooklyn Bridge all in the distance to his right.

Manhattan was in his rear view, the Tri Borough Bridge was to his left and the vast landscape of Queens was in front of him. Normally, he would blast his favorite rap tunes on the car's pull out cassette player and take the expressway home. However at that moment, he needed to think so he just cruised home the long way down Queens Boulevard and other local streets in silence with the radio off. He wanted to clear his mind so he could properly make a decision of what to do next based upon the gravity of the situation he'd just learned of.

He felt cheated and disrespected by Gordon initially because Gordon managed to charm his dying aunt out of who knows how much of the two point five million dollars they won in the settlement. On top of that, he was buying an untold amount of pounds of cocaine with it. Adding injury to total and complete insult, he was selling it back to him. Since Gordon finagled the settlement money from Gwen that he was using to buy wholesale product, in essence Duane actually was buying from himself.

His first immediate thought was to phone Gordon and pretend that he wanted fifty kilos of coke, rob him then kill him and leave him in the Bedell Park Pond. That would serve as a message to show what happens to anyone of violated the new young boss of The Family. The long silent drive in solitude helped to clear his mind so he could begin to think properly. He eventually came to the conclusion that if it wasn't for Gordon, he still wouldn't have a connect for the quality product at the price he was getting it for.

He put himself in Gordon's shoes for a moment and thought what he would have done if a golden opportunity like that fell into his lap. He had to admit to himself that he would have probably done the exact same thing. Only except that he would have probably gotten all of the money out of her then disappeared into thin air. With a sinister grin plastered across his face, he let out a chuckle about the irony of the situation and shaking his head, charged it to the game.

"Well played my man…well played indeed!" Duane said to himself in regard Gordon's strategy.

He got home and later on that night as he and Kiesha watched movies on the V.C.R., then he got the ill fated call. It was his uncle China calling to inform him that his Aunt Gwen had passed away at the hospital a short while earlier. Even though they were separated they'd never gotten an official divorce and China never completely stopped loving Gwen all of the way. In fact the loss of his marriage due to him drinking, drugging, and womanizing was the biggest regret in his life. He came to the hospital at his children's request.

With Paul's hurtful, yet truthful words about having to identify their mother's body and him not being there still ringing fresh in the back of his mind, Duane made up his mind to see to it that his aunt had a proper burial and that he'd be there for the sake of his family. It was very important to him that he be there for his aunt.

He promised to come back to the hospital the very next day. However, as evil as it may seem he just wanted her to die so she would be out of misery and her suffering would be at an end.

Duane had beat up, slashed, stabbed, and shot many people before and had never given a second thought to it. However, seeing his aunt suffer in that manner so close to both his parents dying, it was beginning to be too much for him to bear. His dear aunt Gwen was the only physical link he had left to his mother. Even though Duane only saw Gwen a few times a week once he moved on his own, she looked and acted so much like Winsome with her wavy hair and almond shaped eyes. Now that she was gone, he wouldn't have any one he trusted to turn to for the love that only a mother could provide.

Things were definitely getting crazy and moving way too fast now. However, that's life and you don't get a second chance at it. Up until that time he never knew the effect that cocaine could have on a family. He knew that it was the cocaine she was snorting that made her spend all of their money, or at least that's what he wanted believe. He went through extreme mood swings for several weeks after they laid Gwen to rest. She was cremated and put into the family mausoleum along with his father and mother on Francis Lewis Boulevard.

He made sure that he paid for all the arrangements and got her the biggest flower arrangement as to show how much he loved her. Even without the money Gwen managed to swindle away, at the age of seventeen including the money Gwen did give him Duane had managed to amass a little over two million dollars liquid cash since he'd been home. But even with all that money, he was angry because no dollar amount could bring his parents or his aunt back, no matter what.

In his world, money wasn't everything…it was the only thing, but it still couldn't bring back the dead. The mood swings that he was having after Gwen's death grew worse as the trial date for his gun charges rapidly approached. He went from feeling remorse for his aunt to having a twisted sense of vengeance rationalizing that she got what she deserved for spending all of their money. In short, he was unraveling and rapidly becoming deranged. He still wasn't communicating with his brother either. It was partially out of shame because he didn't want to admit that his brother was right but primarily, he was being pig headed and allowing his pride to get the best of him.

The only thing that gave him just a little bit of focus was his new pet project which was grooming his little cousin P.J. and keeping him out of jail. P.J. who was now fifteen and would soon have a birthday had grown a few inches over the last several years that Duane went back and forth to jail. He was almost eye to eye with Duane who was now five eleven and one hundred seventy five pounds. P.J. had grown to be five nine and one hundred sixty pounds.

P.J. was a magnet for girls with his rugged and exotic good looks. He had his father's slightly slanted eyes, wavy hair and his mothers golden brown completion. P. J. had grown increasingly violent in the time that he lived in Brooklyn. After his mother passed, he acted as if he had cart blanche to act a fool in the street and used her death as an excuse.

Duane had a talk with him and put him back under his wing, He protected PJ as if he was his father instead of China. He would buy P.J. anything as long as he stayed in school and acted civilized, something Duane didn't do himself. It was no disrespect to his uncle but he knew that China had a very long road to recovery from alcoholism. Duane wanted to help his uncle make the transition back to sobriety as easy as possible.

With Gwen dying and China having to move back into the family home in Queens to take care of his children Duane knew that it wasn't going to be an easy task. He just wanted to ease some of the pressure off of his family. Duane made sure that P.J. helped out at the restaurant along with Paul, Dorrine, Mrs. Willcott, and China, who had started working at the restaurant again part time. In addition, he continued to be the super of his building in Brooklyn. He kept his apartment there for when he wanted to entertain his female friends but didn't want to bring them around his children.

Finally, a short while later, the trial for Duane's latest gun charges came up and Kiesha had to testify that she had a valid driver's license at the time that they were pulled over. Mr. Silverman who was now under retainer and represented Duane in all his criminal matters established that since Kiesha's driver's license was valid there was no valid legal reason for the police to search the car. The weapons that Duane admitted were his weren't in plain sight. Silverman contended that the police conducted an illegal search by even going into the car let alone the glove compartment and trunk, which by law, both require a search warrant for the authorities to open them.

He moved to suppress the evidence and told the jury that at best what the police should have done was given them a summons and let them go about their merry way. He also very skillfully and deliberately played the race card. He successfully got under two of the black jurors' skin by saying the police pulled them over simply for no other reason than them being black. One of the jurors was a man and the other was a woman and they appeared to both be in their early to mid forties.

He looked directly into the black woman's eyes and stated "My clients were only pulled over because they were young and black driving an eighty thousand dollar vehicle. If they were white in Bensonhurst, Bay Ridge or say Howard Beach, I know for a fact that the same officers wouldn't have taken a second glance at them. The question remains…are you going to convict my client based on a hunch by these officers that something illegal may have been in that car? If you do, then it's a sad day for justice and you or maybe one of your loved one's very well could be next to fall a victim to these same unfair circumstances."

He closed his argument by citing a technical term "Fruit of a Poisonous Tree" which ties the law's hands if a search and seizer isn't executed properly. If something illegal is found yet it is not specifically stated on the search warrant or the authorities don't have sufficient probable cause to search you, they can't find you guilty. Simply put they can't convict you of something illegal when the method they obtained the evidence against someone was illegal itself. It took the jury only twenty minutes to come back with a not guilty verdict.

Silverman's argument was so concise and emotionally compelling they had no other choice but to find Duane innocent. The black jurors were able to put themselves in Duane's shoes and imagine it was one of them sitting in the driver's seat where Kiesha was when the police pulled them over. The Black woman in her forties imagined that Duane and Kiesha could have easily been her children getting pulled over for no reason and that was enough reasonable doubt for her. Not to mention Silverman's astute assessment of Fruit of a Poisonous Tree. His argument was so good that even the jurors who initially wanted to move toward a conviction had to rule them innocent on those grounds, because they had no other choice.

About a month and a half after the trial, Paul and Raina had a seven and a half pound bouncing baby boy. Paul named him Jarred Jean-Paul Baptiste after his father. Even though the last couple of years had been turbulent for Paul and the rest of the family the future looked bright and very promising. His son was born under the sign of pieces on March the sixth of that year. Ironically, he was born at the exact hospital Winsome worked in before she and Gwen started their business.

CHAPTER ELEVEN

Paul was to graduate from high school in June of that year. He had gotten into St. John's University in Queens that September where he was to play Big East basketball. Since he already owned a home there wouldn't be any need for campus housing and would support himself and his new family by working in the family restaurant until he turned twenty one. That's when he and his brother would receive the other half of the money that Gwen made sure to stash away in a compact interest account before she died. By and by, everything was slowly shaping up for Paul.

As far as Duane's new mode of operations, he was primarily focusing on retailing his product over on Sutton Boulevard and wholesaling outside the projects. His new format was paying off in the form of major dividends for him and his inner circle. Or at least they were until mid June of that year when Duane and Sherman were apprehended as they returned to the projects in Queens from doing business with their Philly connection. Officers from the high intensity drug unit collared Duane and he was hit with an indictment where he was named the head of an illegal drug empire and ordered held immediately.

Both Duane and Sherman were nabbed as they made their way into the projects to watch a high stakes basketball game. Duane had begun to sponsor the Family's summer league since Link and Jerm were locked up. He wanted to be like them so bad that he was finally getting his chance and was ending up just like them. Even though the police came with German Shepherds flashlights and submachine guns when they nabbed him, he still was lucky. Lucky in that the case against him was brought forth by the Queens County D.A.'s office instead of the federal government.

The difference between the state seeking a conviction and the federal government seeking a conviction is that the government normally has a solid case and substantial evidence against you for a period of time where the state may still be building a case and hope to find people willing to flip on you and cooperate with them. It took about a week with both Duane and Sherman being locked up in Queens House of Detention before Mr. Silverman could arrange bail for them. As usual he found a way to bail them out and was paid handsomely for it.

Once Duane hit the street his first order of business was to set up a meeting between him, Donnell and their friends from the Queens South Task Force. They agreed to meet in Five Towns shopping Mall out in Lawrence, Long Island. Lawrence was a suburb of Queens located between Jamaica and Far Rockaway. They always met outside of their district as not to be seen with known criminals. They met in a small diner on Rockaway Boulevard.

"Yo Hinds, what the fuck is up? Why is we payin' you all that money and guys from your unit is the ones that bagged me?" Duane asked angrily.

"Whoa…whoa…whoa! Take it easy and never forget who you're talking to, pal!" Detective Hinds said defensively.

"Yeah…the same muh' fuckers we been payin thousands of dollars to watch our backs so silly shit like this doesn't happen!" Donnell chimed in.

"Take it easy, you! O.K. listen we messed up a little bit and couldn't get in contact with you guys. We been lookin' for you and calling you guys but you guys ain't never there. By the time we tried to call you again it was already too late…they had already picked you up." Detective Pazolli stated.

Knowing that both of them had been in and out of town and not checking their messages Duane just shook his head up and down in agreement then stated.

"O.K. now what happens…can you guys help us out with this one? Cause it's not looking too good for me right now." Duane had regained his composure and calmed down just a little.

"Of course we can help you out but…it's gonna cost you a little bit extra to get a copy of this document we have with all the information we know on it. Now the document doesn't have whosoever ratting on The Family name on it but they specifically name you in it and the rat is listed as a S.O.I. or source of information. I know the two of you are smart guys and probably can figure out exactly who this guy is. Now you didn't hear it from me, but the word is that this guy is the star witness for the D.A.'s office against you. If you could get rid of this guy or persuade him not to testify then the D.A.'s case against you is very weak." Hinds said as he rocked back in the booth they were seated in sipping his coffee.

"Sounds cool…how much we talking about for this document?" Duane quizzed.

"Twenty five large!" Pazolli said without flinching or second guessing the figure.

"You got it on you?" Donnell asked the both of them.

"What's the matter with you…you want it or not? Of course we brought it but let me see the money first!" Hinds shrewdly demanded.

Without another word being uttered Duane went into the trunk of his Jetta and started counting knots of money which he had in a large gym bag. Five minutes later he had the total sum that they requested and gave it to them in a brown paper C-town bag with handles on it. As agreed Pazolli passed them the document in a manila folder after Duane passed him the bag with the knots of money in it. They left the diner and rented a room in a Long Island hotel to thoroughly read over the document.

That way they wouldn't have to worry about N.Y.C. police tailing them since that was out of their jurisdiction. This was the same reason they met Hinds and Pazolli in Lawrence in the first place. That way they wouldn't have to worry about N.Y.C. police tailing them since that was out of their jurisdiction. The same reason they met Hinds and Pazolli in Lawrence in the first place. When they got themselves settled and finally took the document out they couldn't believe how long it was and how much detailed information was compiled on them. In all, it was more twenty pages long and listed Duane, Donnell, and Sherman as the heads of The Family.

"The People of the State Of New York versus Peter "Raw" Baptiste, Donnell Hodges, and Sherman "Shiz" Strom. Hereafter known as the heads of a criminal organization known as "The Family.""

Southern District of New York county of Queens, S.S. :

I, Brian Moore, being duly sworn deposes and says:

I am a detective in the Queens South Task Force assigned to stop the flow of drugs in South Eastern Queens by taking down a criminal enterprise here after referred to as "The Family".

2. There is probable cause to believe that kilograms of powder cocaine, crack cocaine, and heroin will be found on the premises known as Bedell Houses 118-14 New York Boulevard apt. # 8-G Queens, New York 11435.

3. There is also probable cause and or reason to believe that two forty five caliber fire arms that were used in a drug related homicide that an (S.O.I.) who has been reliable in the past says are being held on the premises known as Bedell Houses 118-14 New York Boulevard apt. # 7-F Queens, New York 11435.

The indictment went on for pages but that's all they needed to see to know exactly who was informing the authorities of their activities. Duane's first instincts from before that he didn't want to believe were not only actually right but exact. Now being stopped with Kiesha and his car being searched made perfect sense. He was thanking his lucky stars that they paid Hinds and Pazolli. He was also glad they sold him that document which was going to save him from doing a twenty five to life stretch upstate as a king pin under the Rockefeller drug statutes. Their trial wasn't until mid September so they had plenty of time to take care of who was responsible for giving information to the D.A.'s office.

The party responsible was someone that they'd all known for years and had grown up with. Donnell figured that it was him from the beginning and later when they told Sherman who was ratting on them he almost cried because of who it was. The summer progressed and after that day when Duane and Donnell got a chance to see the actual indictment they acted as if nothing happened, going out and conducting themselves in the same fashion. The only change in their routine was them not hanging out in the projects as much. They knew that this could very well be their last summer in the streets for a very long time so they took pictures as much as possible.

In early September it was agreed that the whole crew including Duane, Sherman, Terry, Junior, Donnell, Ka, Toney, and Khem along with several others would go out to Brooklyn to celebrate Juvert (Ju-Vay). Which was the annual carnival celebrating Labor Day and West Indian heritage held primarily in the Crown Heights and Flatbush sections of Brooklyn. The Carnival starts at sun down and last until the sun rises on Labor Day.

In between the sun rising and setting is the largest street party on the eastern seaboard that happens at the same time and place every year. The crew had all gotten together because this very well may be their last party with all their original members together for a very long time. They did what all the other young men were doing, hanging out in the street drinking beers and heckling young women as the night went on. Everyone was having a good time that evening. Duane had gotten into the festivities so much that he tied two separate bandanas together and wore them on his head.

One bandana had the design of the Haitian flag on it and the other was the Jamaican flag. It's ironic because when he was younger he worked hard to suppress his Caribbean heritage and now he was openly flaunting it. He did it in part to attract all the females who were also of Caribbean descent but also to honor his deceased. This may have been one of the last summer nights he spent free for another twenty five years or better so he decided to let it all hang out.

"Look at this dude D! He fuckin' kills me wearing all that shit like he one of these coconuts…knowing he's as American as apple pie." Terry said aloud to Donnell as he slighty jabbed him in the rib with his elbow to get his attention. They were drinking forty ounce bottles of malt liquor.

"Oh so you got jokes, B? It's cool though don't front like you didn't know my people was from the islands. I'm just showing respect for my heritage and my family man." Duane shot back, still keeping cool.

"Yeah...yeah...yeah, I hear all that jazz you're talkin' but let's just walk up Flatbush and see how many bitches we can pull!" Terry piped in.

They began making their way north on Flatbush Avenue from where they were posted on Caton Ave pushing their way through the very crowded streets that were filled with parade revelers. Terry was drunk and began pushing his way through the crowd a little too hard for a small group of guys that he abrasively brushed past. One of the guys in the group confronted Terry because he said that he stepped on his toes and scuffed his brand new sneakers. Everyone that Terry was with had got lost in the crowd since he was walking so fast bumping through different groups of people.

He was so anxious to walk farther up to where he thought the real action was on Fennimore and Flatbush that the nearest member of his crew was Sherman and he was twenty feet away. Which may as well been twenty miles away by how dense the crowd was that Brooklyn night. There was a tall dark skinned guy wearing a Yankees cap who looked to be in his late teens to early twenties that was in Terry's face arguing with him.

Terry thought that Sherman and the rest of his crew were right behind him. He was so drunk that he didn't realize that everyone had gotten separated.

Terry started arguing back with the guy and he wasn't backing down since he thought everyone was right behind him. Before he could make a move or utter another single word, the tall dark skinned guy in the Yankees cap pulled out a black 357.magnum revolver. He shot Terry directly between his eyes, assassination style at point blank range and once more in his mouth as he fell. The shooter then emptied his four remaining shots in Terry's torso. It was sheer pandemonium once that happened. People began running in all directions trampling each other trying to get away from the bedlam. There was a teenage girl who was in so much shock because she was only two feet away when Terry got murdered. She was catatonic after she wiped away part of Terry's brain and skull fragments and blood out of her hair and off her left arm.

From that moment the crowd heard the first gunshot they started panicking and running in all directions like a Chinese fire drill. Sherman and Duane put their backs to the wall of a barber shop that was closed so they wouldn't get trampled. Everyone else in the crew followed their lead as well until the crowd thinned out enough for all of them to see one another and get to Terry. A whole five minutes had passed before they could see what happened to Terry.

Sherman and Duane were the first to discover Terry's bullet riddled body as they looked at what was left of his face and head and saw his eyes were wide open. It took an ambulance another ten minutes before it could make its way to Terry through all the people walking in the packed to capacity streets. By the time the ambulance got there Sherman had lost it, yelling and screaming at the top of his lungs for the E.M.T.'s to help. It seemed that it just wouldn't register in Sherman's mind that his lifelong comrade was laying there dead on a cold Brooklyn sidewalk and the guy who did it had faded away into the frenzy of the crowd.

"My man…my man…hurry the fuck up and help him! Somebody just shot my man!" Sherman yelled frantically as the men from the ambulance hopped out of their truck with their tools in hand.

Sherman stood right there not wanting to leave his dear friend's side. He couldn't stop staring at him. His white polo shirt was stained with so much blood and gun powder that it looked as if his shirt was never actually white. His eyes lay still with the look of death in them…not how Sherman had seen death in the movies either. He knew that this was a stare into another realm when he looked in Terry's eyes and saw his skull cracked wide open.

The paramedics scraped up what was left of his broken and mangled body that tens of people had stepped on in the confusion. Some of those trying to get away from the gun shots had left footprints on his body. In fact he'd been stepped on so badly that pieces of his flesh were dangling from his arms, legs, and part of his face. The men from the ambulance put him in the back. It was hopeless they knew but Sherman and Duane rode with them to the hospital. They told everyone else that they would see them in the neighborhood the next day.

They were on their way to Kings County Hospital which was normally only five minutes away by car. However, this wasn't any normal day with over two million revelers taking to the streets of Brooklyn to celebrate their heritage. It took the ambulance fifteen minutes to make the five minute drive to the hospital. Terry was pronounced dead on arrival at twelve forty three that morning and sadly enough, he wasn't the only casualty of senseless violence that night at Juvert.

The police came to the hospital and questioned both Duane and Sherman for about an hour before the finally had to let them go. Someone always gets badly hurt or killed the night of the carnival every year so nothing seemed out of place to the detectives of the sixty seventh precinct. The next day back in Queens, people were bar-b-queuing for Labor Day as usual. Only this year there was a huge amount of beer and liquor being poured out on the concrete of Terry's neighborhood in his memory.

Even though everyone was celebrating the holiday, they made it more of a day for Terry who was their latest fallen soldier. People in the neighborhood just couldn't believe how Terry went out. His funeral was held the next Sunday at Gillmont funeral home on Sutton Boulevard not far from where Duane's family's restaurant was located. Duane's contribution to the funeral was having the restaurant cater the wake and going home celebration after the funeral.

Sherman was seemingly the most shook up of the whole bunch of childhood friends. Since Terry was missing half of his head and was so badly mangled, they had no choice but to give him a closed casket service. For Duane, this was the fourth funeral of a loved one or close friend in less than two years. He seemed saddened a bit yet still more resigned than anything, accepting the grim reapers choice to take lives at his beck and call.

The following Wednesday marked the beginning of Duane, Donnell, and Sherman's trial. The Queens County DA wanted a conviction so bad and was so sure that he'd get it one way or another that he was going to be prosecuting the case himself. Mr. Richard A. Baum was on a mission to put away all heads of any drug cartel in his district. He especially had it out for Duane and company because he knew they were affiliated with Link and Germ, but the feds got to them before he could.

Mr. Baum felt embarrassed that the feds came into his district and charged the original members of the family with racketeering, and continuing an ongoing criminal enterprise without him getting a piece of the bust. He was territorial and wanted to prove that he was competent and capable of prosecuting members of organized crime. He wanted to show that he was just as capable as his counterparts in every other borough of the city. He was so cocky, he just knew that he all but had the keys to their cells when he came strutting into the court room.

However, he had a major problem to get around. His star witness was no longer able to testify on behalf of the state against Duane and both his co-defendants. That didn't matter to Baum; he thought the circumstantial evidence would still be enough for him to get a conviction. If by chance it wasn't, he still had a dirty trick up his sleeve as a trump card to give at least one of them jail time. Even if he only got one of them, he wouldn't end up looking like a complete idiot.

Duane showed up wearing a dark blue pin striped Brooks Brothers suit with a white shirt, a burgundy pattern tie and black Gucci wing tipped shoes. He was clean shaven and had a crisp one and a half low fade hair cut. His demeanor was poised yet if you looked closely you could still see the nervousness in his movements. He was, after all, on trial for his life. If the D.A. convicted him of what he and his co-defendants were being accused of, he would receive a mandatory minimum of twenty five years to life without the possibility of parole.

Donnell and Sherman were dressed in pinstriped suits as well, tan and black respectively. Mr. Silverman was appointed by Duane as their attorney as usual. After he got Duane off when he got caught red handed with two guns, Duane was impressed and just short of amazed of Silverman's knowledge of the law. There was no doubt in Duane's mind that he'd get them all out of this latest jam as well.

The trial got under way and lasted two weeks. The D.A. called various police officers and brass to testify extensively about their knowledge of The Family. Every witness that was called to the stand Silverman seemed to be able to quickly tear apart under cross examination. Baum's last chance to get a conviction under the kingpin charges that were bought against Duane and his co-defendants was that he didn't have a documented legitimate source of income. The D.A. contended that there was no way a seventeen year old and his friends could afford such an extravagant lifestyle and have so many luxury cars with no legitimate source of income.

It got to the point that the D.A. was so arrogant about his point that he didn't do his research. Silverman countered the D.A.'s claim about Duane's income by revealing the five million dollar settlement his family had won when his parents were killed. He showed all the documents and receipts for everything that Duane owned. Then he announced that Duane would be receiving another two point five million dollars to split with his brother when he turned twenty one. Silverman took the cake with that move, and demanded that the D.A. stop referring to his clients as drug dealers and criminals.

After deliberating for two days the jury came back with a unanimous innocent verdict. The arrogant and crafty Mr. Baum was vexed beyond any comprehension when the verdict came back. He turned crimson red as he grimaced and loosened his striped tie, almost stomping as he walked out of the court room. There was media coverage on the steps of the Queens County court building. Reporters from all the major stations in the city as well as journalist were present after the verdict was announced. News of the District attorney trying and losing what was supposed to be a slam dunk case was a major spectacle.

Duane and company got into a waiting limo tin front of the courthouse and began celebrating immediately after they were whisked away. They were instructed by Mr. Silverman not to comment to the press. Instead he stayed behind and spoke for them, knowing that his victory directly against the D.A. would boost his already high profile and the rates he charged. Duane was pretty sure that they'd beat the case however, Donnell and Sherman were skeptical.

They were shocked to learn that Duane had secretly been hording millions of dollars without telling them a thing about it. They just knew that their goose was cooked when Baum went for the jugular and asked about their income. Until Silverman came up with those receipts and said Duane bought his friends the cars that they drive they were sweating bullets. Sherman joked and said that he couldn't have written a better ending himself and they went on to party and celebrate their victory and freedom for a whole week afterward.

The following week, Duane's partying came to an abrupt halt when he got a frantic call from Mr. Silverman. "Duane, I'm down here at the court house on Queens Boulevard and I think you better get down here quickly. I don't have the time to explain over the phone… just get down here! I need to see you soon as possible. I'll meet you on the front steps of the courthouse. How long will it take you to get down here?"

"About fifteen minutes, if that…why?" Duane quizzed.

"Because the situation at hand is serious… I mean life or death serious! I'll see you shortly when you get here." Silverman didn't say goodbyes; he then immediately hung up the phone in Duane's face.

"I'll be right back, baby!" Duane told Kiesha as he grabbed the keys to his Saab and walked out the door. Duane didn't know what could be so important. However, when a lawyer who helped you beat illegal weapons charges and a twenty five to life sentence says something is important, then God damn it- it's important! He arrived at the court house about twelve minutes after he got into his car. Once he had a chance to hear what Mr. Silverman had to say, his mind was blown. Paul had been picked up leaving the courts in the projects after a basketball clinic he and Sincere were holding. Police had pulled him over and said that they found an ounce of crack cocaine in the car.

"What are you telling me for? Do what you do and get him off like you be getting me off. Why don't you use that fruity tree thing you said when they found those jammies in my car?" Duane said shrugging his shoulders indifferently.

Silverman was agitated. "You obviously don't know what's going on here! I spoke with D.A. Baum personally and he's an asshole…he said that when they ran your brother's fingerprints and his name they didn't match his, they matched yours! He told me the only criminal record they have of him is the gun charges that you used his name for. Remember that?" Duane knew he was cornered and his nonchalant bravado evaporated. "Simply put, he wants to make a deal. Your brother's freedom in exchange for you doing some time on impersonating charges…what do you say to that offer?" Silverman's manner was matter of fact, as though even he knew this time, it was a wrap.

"Fuck Silverman, you can't just get him off like you always do for me?" Duane asked nervously. He could handle being put under tremendous pressure to make such a decision on the spot.

"It's not that easy, I'm afraid. Listen, after what happened last week…I know this guy Baum personally and he already hates my friggin' guts…with a passion! We go way back to sixty nine when he was just a snot nosed young punk trying cases way before he ever dreamed of being the D.A. . He wants to make a deal and he's downstairs waiting in his office right now. You want to speak to him?" Silverman probed.

"I got a funny feeling about this shit man and I don't like it one bit, but fuck it let's go see what this faggot muh' fucka is talking about." Duane said prepared to meet whatever fate that rested on the other side of the district attorney's office door. He thought strategically and realized he was in a bad spot. Baum could snake him and arrest him for the impersonation charges then turn around and still charge Paul. If he could at least get Paul out of it that would be one win – at least. They went through several metal detectors before Duane and Ira Silverman made the left that led down the stairs to the D.A.'s office and discovered him fixing his brown toupee when they walked in.

"So Peter...or is it Paul today?" He had a mirror in his hand, nonchalantly adjusting his rug as he spoke. When he thought he had it perfect, he leaned back in his seat and cracked a smile."You didn't think you were just going to make me look like a complete imbecile at trial and get off totally scot fucking free did you? Nah... nah...nah...it doesn't quite work like that. No little street punk makes an ass out of Richard A. Baum...no, not a street punk...not any one!" The D.A. now clenched his fists, pacing the floor methodically and slowly back and forth before retaking a seat at his desk.

"You're just full of surprises though aren't you? First the millions of dollars… then I find out you have an identical twin brother. You got over on me, kid…big time! But now I got you by the balls, son…by the balls!" The D.A.'s face was covered with a devilish grin and he stared directly at Duane as if he were shooting daggers out of his eyes directly through him.

"Mr. District Attorney could you please explain to us why my client should take such a deal when he's totally legitimate? Besides I sincerely question the legality of the search of my other client's vehicle." Silverman stated.

"Because, I'll make the lives of him and his family a living hell that's why! I'll say the the restaurant that your family owns was started by illicit funds. I'll keep your brother away from his new born son and give each and every member of your family parking tickets every time they step out of a vehicle. If any member of your family breathes the wrong way I'll have them arrested and ran through the system. See after I found out that you had a twin I did my research on your whole family…trust me I'll make it hard for them to breath if you don't co-operate with the forgery charges!" Baum's intentions were nothing less than diabolic.

"That's ridiculous. You can't prove their restaurant was started with illicit funding! I'll mop the floor with you or any of your young maverick A.D.A.'s if you even try to bring that foolishness into a court of law." Silverman said in response to Baum's threats.

"That may be true, but I'll have them closed down and tied up in red tape for a year before you can prove otherwise. Ira, you've known me for over twenty years…you know if anything I can get anal with the best of them!" Baum retorted.

Knowing that Baum could indeed be an asshole, Silverman took him seriously and asked.

"Alright let's say we do the deal…can my other client make bond immediately?" Silverman asked.

"Nah…no dice, I need this quid pro quo! Excuse the pun, but I want Peter in exchange for Paul!" Baum said vehemently.

"But under what grounds are you denying Paul's bond? He's got ties to the community, he's starting his freshman year at St. Johns in a few weeks and he just had a son. I see no legitimate reason for you to hold him without bond…come on Richard, just be reasonable about this." Silverman stated as he pleaded for leniency for his young clients.

"He's being held with no bond because he's a flight risk, that's why!" The D.A. stated before being cut off by Mr. Silverman.

"A flight risk come on, give me a break already... you're really reaching aren't you?" Silverman asked.

"No, Ira actually, not at all. Remember he has access to millions of dollars and he wasn't born in this country. Oh, I did my research on these guys this time and found out that they were supposed to have been born in Jamaica. That's good enough reason for me to hold him as a flight risk until we can schedule a trial. If you fuck with me I'll see to it that his trial isn't until six months away. I really don't want to Ira, but you know me...I'll do it." Baum stated eyeballing Duane.

"Let me speak to my client for a moment in private...if that's alright with you, Richard." Silverman was clearly aggravated by the circumstances but he wouldn't give Baum the satisfaction of knowing how trapped he felt his clients were. He still kept his poker face until Baum checked something on his desk and then left.

"I'm sorry, kid he's got us backed into a corner on this one. It's all up to you if you want to take the deal or not. If you want, we can see if he'll give you twenty four hours or so to make up your mind." Silverman looked helpless as if his hands were tied. He tried to soothe Duane's nerves at the same time. He knocked on the door and Baum came back in, not caring if they'd thought he'd been eavesdropping on the other side because of course, he had.

"O.K. says he takes the deal. Can he have twenty four hours to get his affairs together? And how much time is on the table here anyway?" Silverman asked.

"A year and one day!" Baum said with a straight and impassive face.

"Come on that's the maximum for that in this case isn't it? Can't you be a little more lenient, Richard?" Silverman asked.

"No…the way I see it that's only a small price to pay for making me look like an ignoramus at trial. In fact, the totality of the deal I have in place is for him to do the year and a day at a state facility then be turned over to the I.N.S. to be deported on forgery charges." Baum said.

"Bastard…what's that going to do?" Silverman asked furiously.

"Well counselor it'll give me something that I didn't have since I lost the case to you…peace of mind! See I don't care if your client conducts his affairs in Kings County, Bronx County, New York County (Manhattan), or even Richmond County (Staten Island) for that matter. I won't have any cocaine cowboys running around getting rich and flaunting it in my face! No not in Queens County and certainly not on my watch! That's the deal I'm offering. You have until this time tomorrow to accept it, take it or leave it! If you leave it Paul will be on Riker's Island until it's time for his trial." Baum flatly stated.

That concluded their conversation that evening. Faced with a decision that could hurt all the remaining members of his family, Duane's head was swimming. What if the D.A. is bluffing? He thought to himself. Six months isn't that long on Riker's. Then he came to his senses knowing his brother wasn't even remotely built for jail. The sharks and piranhas in there would make fish food out of him.

He defiantly didn't like being squeezed by the D.A. one bit, however, he thought back to the conversation he had with Sincere the day he left to get his own apartment. Sure enough his dirt had caught up to him and was about to effect every one he loved if he didn't take the deal. Death, hell, and destruction…those three words Sincere said were now ringing loudly in Duane's head. He thought about the deaths of his parents, aunt, and Terry. He saw the hell he put his family through with his antics and now if he didn't make the right decision he could destroy the lives of his immediate family and loved ones.

By the time he made it back to his apartment, he knew he'd do the honorable thing and take the miserable deal the Queens County D.A. was offering. Duane wasn't a dummy in his heart of hearts he could see that the D.A. had this set up all along. He figured that it was a backup plan way before he even stepped into the courthouse for his last trial. He came into his apartment and gave Kiesha the bad news. He then went to see Donnell and Sherman a little while later and told them what happened.

They both vowed to take care of his belongings and make sure to visit him and to also make sure he had whatever he needed while he was in jail. Even though he was so young, they genuinely appreciated how he carried himself as a boss, and first and foremost a man. They also loved how he stuck his neck out for them at their trial by saying he purchased all of their flashy materials with his case money. This in turn allowed them to all keep their freedom.

The next morning he found his little cousin P.J. and told him the staggering news. They hung out for a short while before P.J. had to go to school and he gave him instructions to behave himself. He told P.J. now that he was more than likely going to be deported that he had to be the strength of the family until he could find his way back from Jamaica. He went on to say good bye to his uncle China and Mrs. Willcott then went home and made sweet love to Kiesha for the last time until he could return. Then, at six that evening he went and turned himself into the district attorney with both Kiesha and Mr. Silverman by his side. As agreed, Paul was released and the bogus charges against him were dropped. Duane was immediately remanded into the custody of the state and the pompous district attorney got his way.

As far as the facility Duane would end up doing his time in, Silverman was at least able to broker a deal for him to do his time in Queens Borough, a state facility located on Van Dam Street in the Long Island City section of Queens. Being as though Baum was going to turn him over to the I.N.S. and he'd be deported to a country that he really knew little about, Silverman said that at least this way he'd still be close to friends and family. Because once the I.N.S. snatched him there'd be no telling where they'd keep him or how long it would be for him to get deported.

Even though, Duane was only about a few weeks shy of his eighteenth birth day he lived almost ten life times in that short period. Mentally, he thought and felt like he was thirty five. He lived the life he chose, and loved...and he lived it very well! Now he'd give his brother a chance to begin his life and live it with his brand new family. Live for his new born nephew whom he hadn't seen yet, because of him being pig headed and stubborn.

There were a lot of things that were going to be resolved by him making the decision to turn himself in. This was his way of bringing back some honor to his family that he felt he'd shamed. It was also a way of telling his brother that he was right about the argument they had without saying so and hearing Paul gloat. Even though, that wasn't his brother's character anyway, Duane's pride and ego wouldn't let him risk it.

He started making plans of what he'd do with all the money when he got back home to Southside. He had the one point five million in reserve for when he turned twenty one, not to mention the roughly two million in cash that he had stashed away. Minus of course the two hundred thousand that he left his uncle to take care of the family and to get him back into the country when the time was right. He also had to thank his lucky stars that his parents said that he was born in Jamaica instead of Haiti because he couldn't speak a bit of French or Creole. He figured that Jean must have known something like this was going to happen and prepared his son without him even knowing. He wasn't happy about going to jail, yet he was a bit anxious to see what waited on the shores of Jamaica for him.

In the wake of Duane being incarcerated, Donnell and Sherman found a new connect in New York. They decided to take their show on the road to Philly, D.C., Baltimore, Newport News, Virginia Beach, and Hampton Virginia. New York and especially Queens had become too hot for them after the arrest of Duane. They knew if they got caught doing anything the D.A. would throw them under the jail.

Once in a while they'd have a laugh about how good of an acting job Sherman did the night Terry got killed and at his funeral. They'd joke that he should have won an academy award. They had used a hit man from East New York that Ka knew. They'd given him the pictures they were taking all summer so he'd have a fresh picture of who to hit. Duane put the order out for him to be executed at Juvert knowing people randomly get shot there every year. He made that decision after they found out that he was the D.A.'s snitch from the affidavit they bought from the police. Donnell was right on the money not to like or trust Alex from Rosenberg Village as well.

As it turns out Alex got caught trying to transport thirty kilos of coke into Hartford, Connecticut during a stop for a broken headlight. He was mad that Link and Germ took so much of his money from the high steaks bets during the basketball games and that they never game him a break when he'd re-up. That made it much easier for him to tell the federal government who his supplier was.

When Alex's trial came up, the government found him not to be a credible witness and sentenced him two natural life sentences to be run concurrently. He was immediately remanded to the Otisville Federal Correctional Facility where he was killed the first day he got there. Link and Germ got word that he was the rat on their federal beef and had a couple of their associates who was already serving life poke him up well over seventy times with a fork and ice pick that they smuggled out of the kitchen. Later that year, Silverman got Link and Germ's case overturned on a technicality and brought them home on appeal.

Overall, even though Duane found himself in a horrible situation he was proud of all the things that he was able to come through as well as the genuine and good people he had in his corner, like his parents and Sincere. Now that he found himself back in a cell he had nothing but time to think. The last talk that he'd had with Sincere resonated in his head as he reminisced on what he said.

"Son every man must go through his own personal trials and tribulations in life because that's what makes us stronger as men. In some cases it even makes us who we are. Every man must learn from these experiences so he can have his own understanding about life. But you can't give a man understanding- he has to get it himself. Those of us who are fortunate find understanding in what...time. Some aren't fortunate and go through life never understanding what the science of life is all about at all!"

Duane knew that he was down on his luck however he tried to look at his situation optimistically. Maybe he was in this situation that looked bleak and he was actually one of the fortunate ones Sincere spoke of. Maybe he'd finally have an understanding of life instead of always trying to be understood. Either way even though, he was now working with less than crumbs. He knew that one day soon he'd be back to not only take the cake but the whole bakery.

FIN

A SNEAK PEEP OF MAXWELL PENN'S EROTIC TALE

"The Jezebel Chronicles: Odyssey of a Whore"

There was no more to be said with just mere words alone. The mystical essence of attraction which lovers share had been in the air all evening. Now that they both were certain that this was to be, what once only existed as potential was definitely, rapidly becoming a reality. Their eyes were interlocked. The either which comprised the very air they were breathing made the atmosphere seem as if it actually were on fire!

Without losing the electric glare that they both were sharing, they simultaneously began to rise slowly from behind Ka's creamy white baby grand piano where they'd been sitting. Ka started to take charge and went for Jessica's arm to pull her into his embrace. All the while, he marveled at her luxurious, even-toned, Godiva dark chocolate complexioned skin. He traced the symmetrically statuesque contours of her winsome face, his desires focused on her ravishing five foot six Nubile frame.

Jessica took a step back and slightly bumped the piano. Almost knocking over what was left of the bottle of Dom P and both flutes that they'd been drinking from. Their vibe was so intense she couldn't worry about being embarrassed. She wanted to really and truly savor this monumental moment for all eternity. She thought that Ka may have been in a tad bit more of a rush than she would have liked him to be.

This was the only time where in her view the eight year age difference between them may have shown, if only just a glimpse. Her mind was racing with so many thoughts. Her heart pumped adrenalin through every square inch of her body. She felt butterflies in her stomach and the electricity between them tingled all the way to the tips of her French manicured fingers. Was he in a slight rush because he desired her the same way that she had been secretly lusting after him?

Night after night, she touched herself all over her body in her special places, bringing herself decadent pleasures, hoping, wishing and dreaming it was him. It didn't matter what part of his body was touching her. As long as it was him, it didn't matter. Yes, him and him alone- that was all that really mattered. Whether it was his strong brown sturdy masculine hands, his lips, or his tongue, let alone his juicy rod. She just shuttered to think how good of a lay and a stud her young lover would be.

Internally her juices were beginning to flow like Victoria Falls. Three months passed since Pasquale introduced them that night in the club. Even though she acted a bit coy and had been juggling several other men, Ka was the singular object of her utmost inner desires. A woman of her stature couldn't just say she wants to take you back to the Kasbah and hump for days on end… even if that's what she really wanted to do. She had to show a little more poise and restraint with him.

She slowly took a few steps back from the piano bench. She wanted to make sure she didn't accidentally bump the piano again. She also purposely stood back as to make Ka come to her. Just as she thought he would, Ka took two paces toward her. Only to be stopped by the softness of Jessica's inner left palm. She stood there with the tips of her left fingers gently and methodically tracing the outline of Ka's six pack abs which were so well pronounced you could see them through the Simi loose form fitting black V-neck cashmere sweater he was wearing.

Just as Ka was about to utter a statement, Jessica made a shushing notion with her right hand, seductively placing her index finger in front of her full pouty supple lips. Then, with the back of the same hand she began to caress the left side of his ruggedly handsome face while persuasively bringing her index finger once again to the center of her lips in her most sensual tone saying, "Relax baby…I can feel the tension in your stomach. Don't be nervous. We have all evening… the night is still young. Why don't you turn the stereo on and play something we can both unwind to?"

Ka just chuckled, revealing a confident, all telling and mischievous grin. Then he clasped her left hand which was just massaging his core and began leading her to his king sized bed.

Same Blood Different Veins:
By Frederick Chapple

As Jewels and Gutta made their way to hook up with this cat in North Philly to conduct the transaction he drove through Diamond Street where the hood was still the hood. Kids playing basketball on crates, little girls jumping double Dutch rope, young niggas eyes glared with envy while the Ghetto gold diggers begged for attention from the occupants of the Cadillac truck. Jewels Grew up there and still considered that area home.

"Why you drivin' through here dog?" Gutta questioned Jewels. "We got shit to take care of nigga!"

"Man I'm just gonna drop this change off to this broad real quick and we out." Jewels replied to Gutta.

Gutta's problem with the pit stop was due to the fact that they were ridin' dirty. Its rules to the drug game but Jewels had rarely followed any of them because he lived by his own rules. Even though Kayla was exclusively his, he did his thing on the side. He had a different meaning for the word faithful. He figured as long as he spent time with her, told her that he loved her and provided the materialistic things she wanted to keep her happy then nothing else really mattered. He was definitely going to continue to do him. "FUCK BITCHES-GET MONEY" was tatted across his back in Celtic old English lettering to co-sign his player facade.

He pulled over alongside the curb and beeped the horn. A pretty face peeped through the curtains of the window to the row house he pulled in front of. A few seconds later the door opens and an extremely bad ass light-skinned chick exited onto the side walk. She walked over to the trucks driver driver's side smiling from ear to ear. With each step she took the sway of her hips and the switch of her shapely robust ass spoke volumes. Once she stood in her bow-legged stance her image could have turned the gayest man on the planet straight.

"Hey Jewels." She said batting her pretty brown eyes.

"Here, Kia." Jewels said as he handed her some cash. "I'll holla at you later on, I gotta go handel some business right now."

"Ah'itght." She responded, kissed him then turned and waked away toward the house as Gutta focused on her slinky stride.

"Damn! Shorty got a fat lil' ass on her!" Gutta blurted out unable to keep the comment to himself.

Jewels just looked at his cousin, smiled and then poped his collar. Gutta turned the volume back up in the truck and reclined his seat way back while Jewels muscled his way back into traffic. Minutes later the truck pulled up right outside of the 27th St. lounge. Jewels cuts the engine off as Gutta reached for his cell phone and began to dial a number.

"Yeah, I'm in front of the bar on 27th St." Gutta speaks into the phone. "Ah'ight hurry up!"

Those were the last words to come from Gutta's mouth before seeing the bright flash of light out the corner of his right eye. BOC! The loud gunshot was the last thing he heard before everything became silent to him. Before Jewels could react his cousin's brain was all over him and his dashboard. BOC! BOC-BOC! Shots just kept continuing to ring out, filling the truck with metal and bullet holes.

Jewels ducked down beneath the steering wheel as he drew his black double action forty caliber, aiming it in the direction of the shooter. Jewels squeezed his trigger a few times. Just as the shooting had started it stopped just like that. When the smoke cleared Jewels slowly stuck his head up and looked around. The streets were a ghost town. The doors of the bar swung open and patrons began to peep out the witness the aftermath of what had took place.

Gutta was slumped over with his head resting on the dash as his brains oozed out the large hole on the side of his head. He wasn't moving, he was motionless, breathless…lifeless all in a fraction of a second less than a blink of an eye. Jewels shook his cousin but in his heart he knew that it was of no use. Frantically he started up the truck, peeling off in route to the hospital in hopes of getting Gutta some help.

Jewels grabbed his cell phone and called the police as he moved the big toy through traffic. Realizing that his own flesh and blood was already gone for good the thought of the bricks of drugs and his gun inside the truck made him pull over and stash everything in an alley. After he threw the spent shell casings of his gun from the truck, he continued on to the hospital. He knew the police would want to check his truck and questioning him for hours wasn't that far behind.

For info on Maxwell Penn his latest books and appearances
log on to:

www.sincerecommgroup.com
www.myspace.com/maxwellpennonline
Maxwellpenn@facebook.com
Maxwellpenn@twitter.com

0r call (917)915-5641